The Decaying Pillars

I0453060

Journalism is corrupt. This is its story.

"The speed of communications is wondrous to behold. It is also true that speed can multiply the distribution of information that we know to be untrue."

-Edward R. Murrow

Steve Ruygrok

Edited by Kathleen Dale

Cover by Aldo Corona

Chapter 1

In a coffee shop in downtown Newbury, Eric Peterson took a sip of his espresso. A woman walked inside and saw Eric from across the cafe. She set her briefcase down and the two shook hands.

"Hello, Ms. Piersen, please take a seat."

"Thank you, Eric," she said.

Eric, who worked out at the gym regularly, was wearing a black suit with a tie and had sunglasses that sat on top of his head, pointed to the barista. "Did you want a coffee or anything?"

Gwen adjusted her white blouse. "No thanks. Are you ready to begin the interview?"

"Straight to business. I am ready."

She held up her recorder toward Eric. "Did you think that just because you're a billionaire, no one would care about how you abused the journalism industry?"

Eric smiled. "The Times was a business designed to make money, and it did. Outside of that, nothing else matters to me."

"You've seen the fallout, Eric. Does the collusion, deception, and what you call native advertising bother you now that The Times is dead?"

Without hesitation, Eric replied, "When we started back in 2006, journalism was a gazelle waiting for a lion to tear it to pieces. You people got lazy and didn't see the opportunities for what they were. The Times changed this business forever, and it's the reason why your paper is one of the only ones left."

Gwen glared at Eric. "And what about Jack Strain? What has become of him? No one knows what he's doing now."

"Jack Strain was the mastermind. He was the man who led The Times, championed native advertising, and saw to it that no other company would come within a mile's length of The Times' success." Eric took a sip of espresso. "What's funny to me is how you people in New York still embrace native advertising, even after everything it has done."

Gwen put the recorder down. "We may use it as a business model, but you can bet your ass that if we had any alternative, we would use that instead."

"Would you?"

Gwen got up from her chair and was about to leave when she turned around. "Jack Strain is the reason this industry is dead." She walked out of the cafe.

Eric took a sip of his coffee and looked at Gwen as she left. "Fool, you owe Jack Strain more than you can imagine."

Eric lined up his tie and tightened it while he sat in The Times' office as he waited for Jack Strain to arrive for his interview. "The day has come to shake things up," he said as he saw Jack walk into the office.

They shook hands and sat down.

Eric looked at Jack, who had a shaggy goatee and was slightly overweight. "It's a pleasure to finally meet you, Jack. I've heard so much about you."

"Likewise."

He folded his hands on the table. "So, do you think you have what it takes to lead The Times? Before you say yes, know that this isn't the journalism you've been used to."

Jack smiled. "You know what, Eric? I spent eight years at World Line Magazine as Editor-In-Chief. I took it from an unknown voice to a global authority. I did that with boundaries and restrictions, but here at The Times, in online media, rules can be bent, manipulated, and sometimes broken. Forgiveness comes easy online and we will use that to our advantage."

Eric glanced at a piece of paper on the desk. "So tell me what you think about article headlines?"

"I think they are undervalued and underused. Too many people see them as boring labels to separate one article from another, but I see them as a drug. I see headlines as something that will keep readers coming back again and again, even when their minds are telling them no. Online media is about generating a reaction from the reader. It's about invoking unexpected emotions."

Eric looked again at the paper. "What about accuracy and timeliness?"

"Fine if we can have them."

He looked up at the ceiling for a moment. "What is the future of journalism?"

Jack laughed. "There is no future for journalism. For online media and writing, the future is unknown, yet bright."

"My wife Jessica once told me, being ethical prevails above all else and I agree. However, being ethical should be done on a calculated basis. After all, it's only a word."

"And one that is becoming less and less important these days," Jack said while nodding.

Eric leaned forward with a smile. "So what is your vision for The Times?"

"The way I see it, we're in 2006, the industry is ours to seize. There is a natural progression to building up a news website and we will complete it. Once we are big enough, we will blaze a trail no one has ever seen. We will establish a business that is sustainable. The naysayers will eat their words and swallow their pride when they look up at what we have become. The Times will be the best, and nothing but that will suffice."

Eric extended his hand. "I knew you were the man for the job."

A week later, the two met back in The Times' office. Eric sat in the conference room with Jack.

Eric pointed at the TV. "My team of researchers recently did a study on the behavior of online readers: what their tendencies are, what they like, what they don't like, what they can forgive, and what they never will. The bullets you see above are to be the pillars of what The Times is about."

Jack look bewildered. "It just says traffic, revenue, and traffic."

"Exactly."

"Okay, understood."

Eric handed Jack a piece of paper. "Jack, these are the people who will be your editors. We'll bring them in so you can meet them, get a feel for their personalities, but they've each been selected for a reason. They don't know they've been hired, but they have. Get a feel for each person and welcome them to The Times. The site officially goes live this January."

"Okay, anything else?"

Eric looked at Jack. "Here is the new style guide, make sure your editors accept and embrace it." He shuffled some papers together. "I'd say good luck, but I don't think you need it."

A third party agency helped fill the open positions at The Times. In total, there were 50 employees working for the outlet.

The first individual Jack interviewed was a young, black man named Cameron Nelson, who had been serving as Editor for a local newspaper in Dallas for four years. The two of them sat down and Jack peeked at his resume. "Why should you get this job?"

Cameron stumbled to answer, caught off guard. "My experience speaks for itself, and so does the work I've done. I generate the most compelling, hard news money can buy. My work is undeniable."

"That it is, Cameron." Jack scratched his forehead. "Why do you want to work at The Times? What about this place is attractive? We're a brand-new site, why come here?"

Cameron nodded. "I came to The Times because print journalism is dying. My outlet is laying off people left and right, and business doesn't feel like it'll improve. I know online is the future for journalism and I want to be a part of that future from the start. Newbury is a great place to live and businesses run by Eric Peterson have always been successful."

Jack handed him The Times' style guide. "Take a look through the first page and its bullets. This is how we'll ultimately do things, what do you think about that?"

Cameron looked through the page thoroughly. "Some of this is unethical, Jack, you know this. You want me to tell you I'll be fine ignoring the ethics of journalism on a whim, right?"

Jack smirked.

"Well, let me tell you that when the time comes, I won't have to. Quality journalism beats shady reporting any day of the week." Cameron crossed his arms.

Jack thought for a moment. "I know you're going to do great things for us, Cameron. The credibility you'll bring will be essential, and after we've built The Times up, then we can address your thinking."

"Or you'll be of the same mind."

Jack stood up and shook his hand. "Congratulations, Cameron. Welcome to The Times."

Cameron left the office.

Jack took a sip of coffee as his secretary called in the next candidate, Jill Reddick. Jill, a white, middle-aged woman sat down in front of Jack's desk.

"Hello, Ms. Reddick. Tell me, why do you want to work here? Why work with a start up website?"

She folded her hands in her lap. "Well, Jack. I'm here because every print outlet I've ever worked for has had nothing but sexist, male assholes for bosses and I'm tired of being treated as an inferior just because of my gender. I believe I am a great journalist and can do wonderful things for The Times."

Jack looked serious. "I don't care if you're male, female, black, white, Asian or Mexican. The only thing I care about is results. Can you get me results, Ms. Reddick?"

"Yes, I can. I can learn and adapt better than anyone. Whatever direction we go, I'm all in."

Jack glanced at her resume on his desk. "I spoke with your last boss, you know. He told me he fired you for insubordination, said you threw his computer up against the wall. That's an interesting way to treat your boss."

Jill took a deep breath. "Yes, all of that is true, but the man deserved far worse if you ask me."

"Pity, I would've thrown him out the window," Jack said, smiling.

Jill laughed. "Well, he didn't deserve that."

"A kind heart. I like that." Jack slid the style guide across the table to her.

Jill looked at it. "I'm fine with this."

Jack stood up to shake hands with Jill as he welcomed her to The Times, then she left.

He looked at his phone and saw Eric had texted him. "How's it going?"

"As planned," Jack replied. He put the phone back in his jacket.

Jack's secretary called in the next candidate, Dustin Smith. He was a young, fit Asian-American man who worked as an editor in Los Angeles. Dustin took his seat. "J-Strain, D-Smith. It's a pleasure."

Jack stared at him.

Dustin whistled. "You there?"

"Yes, I am, the name is Jack." He shuffled some papers on his desk. "Why do you want to work for The Times?"

Dustin slapped his leg. "Come on Jacky-poo, you know why. I'm going to get views for breakfast, lunch, and dinner. I'll crank out traffic like I-80 at five o'clock in the evening on a week night."

"You lost me at come on."

"Well then come find me, Jacky. Listen, all you need to know is I will rock this job like a Metallica concert in July," Dustin said with an eyebrow raised.

Jack stared at Dustin and took a deep breath. "Here's our style guide." He handed it over to him.

Dustin took a moment to look at it. "Copy that."

"Copy what?" He shook his head. "Just tell me yes if you're able to work within those guidelines."

"I got this."

"I know you," Jack motioned quotes with his hands, "got this. I just want to hear you say yes. A yes, one word, nothing else."

"Si."

"You know we're in Amer…" Jack looked away. "Just, you're hired."

Dustin stood up. "Jacky!" He motioned for Jack to hug him. "Bring it in. Get some Dusty love, get some."

"I'll get none." Jack pointed at the door. "It was nice to meet you. I know you'll do great things for us."

"Like Picasso did paintings," Dustin said as he walked out of the office.

Jack sat down. "Yikes."

He pulled out his phone again and texted Eric. "That was a weird one. You sure Dustin is the man for the job?"

"Yes of course, he is highly skilled, despite the weirdness," Eric replied.

Jack was ready and his secretary called in the final candidate. Her name was Karen Drove, a young and beautiful light-skinned woman. She served as an editor for a global magazine for six years. Karen came into his office and took a seat.

"Hi, Karen, how are you?"

"I'm doing well, thank you for asking."

Jack threw his hands up in the air. "You're normal, thank the lord."

"I'm sorry?"

Jack put up his hand. "Oh, my apologies, it's just nice to meet someone who communicates like a normal person."

Karen looked around the room.

"So, Ms. Drove, why do you want to join The Times?"

"The magazine I worked for closed, so I lost my job. My brother and his family are here and even though there aren't many job opportunities in Newbury, I decided to move anyway. I was contacted by a friend who said Eric Peterson was starting up an online news website and that the company wanted to interview me, so here I am."

Jack leaned forward. "Do you know what we're doing here? You understand what The Times will be?"

"Yes, I do. I need the job and want to live here, so I'm willing to ignore my journalistic reflexes."

He smiled as he handed her their style guide. "Then I don't need to ask you if you have any problems with this."

"No, you don't."

Jack sat back in his chair. "Fantastic. You got the job, but you already knew that when you came in here, didn't you?"

Karen stood up and shook his hand. "I did." She left Jack's office.

He took his phone back out to text Eric. "Cameron and Karen seem resistant, why did you pick them again?"

"Trust me, they are essential," Eric replied.

Chapter 2

It was the beginning of January 2007 and The Times' first day had arrived. Jack was the first one in the building that morning, so he hung up a few pictures in his office as well as his college degree.

After he was all set up, he walked around and saw where his four editors, Cameron, Jill, Dustin, and Karen, would be stationed. He then went to the kitchen to brew up some coffee. Jack gazed out into the metropolitan skyline of downtown Newbury as he wondered what the future would hold. A gorgeous morning sun was rising in front of him, as it casted a magnificent color on the buildings below.

Slowly but surely people started to trickle in, and shortly after, Jack called a company meeting in the common area. Eric had set up a small stage against one of the walls for when the whole company needed to be addressed.

Jack stood on the stage and looked around the crowded room. "Ladies and gentlemen, this is The Times. All of you are the foundation for the phoenix that will rise and tower over journalism, online media, and all news. Our content will be irresistible, our audience's thirst for The Times will be insatiable. We will be the absolute best this industry has and will ever see. Get ready to succeed, people. We are about to blaze a trail no one will see coming." Jack paused. "Ladies and gentlemen, welcome to The Times."

After his speech, Jack asked his editors to meet him in the editorial conference room. They all took their seats and looked up at Jack, who was dressed in khakis and a flannel button-down shirt.

He sat with his hands folded. "Everyone here has been chosen for a reason. I expect The Times to dominate this industry. Do not feel shackled by the old model of journalism's past. You have our style guide. Use it, embrace it, live it. I want each of you to invent and innovate. Destroy any barriers of creativity that lie before you."

Cameron raised his hand. "But do so ethically, right?"

Jack shook his head as the silver chain around his neck moved. "Creativity is king here, Cameron. Ethics can wait, traffic cannot." He leaned forward. "Find me the best news, find it for me now."

Cameron sat back in his chair, looking around the room for someone to say something, but no one did.

Karen looked through the style guide as she bit her nails. "What are the production numbers we're aiming for and how soon should we expect to see them?"

He pointed at a piece of paper. "Soon, Karen. Just know, the faster we grow, the better it will be for all of us."

Jill adjusted her large framed glasses. "About the bullet point regarding headlines. We don't want to put anything in there that isn't in the story, right?"

"Yes and no," Jack said, nodding. "It's important to express the current facts, but couple that with what the future might hold. Ask the reader a question. Above all else, your headline should stir up emotions within the reader. If they are apathetic about your story from the start, how far do you think they'll get reading your article?"

Jill looked back at him. "Not far."

"Exactly. This is online, people. In print, facts had to be confirmed prior to publishing, but in online, facts can be confirmed after. Run with a lead and correct as you need to. If precision and accuracy are available in a story, always see that it's done, but don't feel confined to the old way of doing things."

Karen said, "But our credibility is everything. If we report something false, our readers will abandon us."

"If we are wrong consistently, yes," Jack said as he turned his head. "You are some of the best reporters around and you were brought in because of your reputation. People trust you and your names. Our credibility will be rock solid from the start."

Cameron held up the style guide. "Readers won't forgive this."

"That's just it, readers will forgive it. The online nature of the world today has enabled us to be wrong every once in a while. Things happen at a mile per second and there's too much happening for people to dwell on one false report."

They all sat there thinking for a moment.

Jack leaned forward in his chair. "If you have a question, just ask. We're all on the same team. You all ready now?"

Dustin, who wore an "I rock the party" t-shirt, grinned. "Ready, Jack? I don't get ready. Ready gets me."

Jill looked at him, puzzled. "What does that even mean?"

Karen smiled. "We got it, Jack. We're ready."

They all walked out of the room and got to work.

From that day forward, Jack relied on his team to generate interesting stories that had unique angles.

At a meeting six months in, Jack updated his team on their progress. "We are half a year in and are seeing unprecedented growth. The combination of great content, a satisfying user experience, effective ads, and improved rankings in search engines has helped us become one of the most viewed sites in the country."

Cameron looked up at Jack. "So keep doing everything we've been doing?"

"Absolutely. Currently, we are sitting at 10th overall in national traffic, but we can do better."

The Times' largest producer of traffic was Cameron, and he captured his audience through classic, hard-hitting news. Later that day, Jack walked over to Cameron's desk to discuss his traffic.

Jack took a seat. "Cameron, through solid, quality content you've helped us earn one of the highest search engine rankings, but we need to start taking advantage of it. I know you're doing hard news, but this meeting is about getting you to step outside of the norms of journalism."

Cameron sat straight up. "All those things you just said are true, so why do I need to change? I see no reason to do anything differently."

Jack shuffled some papers he had with him. "It's definitely important to continue to produce quality content, but consider some alternatives." He set down a traffic report in front of Cameron. Jack pointed to the report. "At a very basic level, headlines are the gateway to a highly read article, as you know. Some of your headlines have been vague when they could have been more specific. Headlines are prime places for speculation and that is where forward-looking speculation can be inserted. For example, 'United Nations Summit Results In Turmoil And Dissention.' That's a nice headline and would probably get decent traffic, but you know what would really make it pop? 'United Nations Summit Results In Bitter Turmoil, War On The Horizon?' Do you see what I did there, Cameron?"

Cameron turned his head. "I see what you did, but was the second half of the headline about war something that was factually possible?"

"War is always possible, Cameron."

Cameron's eyes wandered around the room.

Jack pointed to another part of the report. "In our A&E section, a different example could be, 'Cruz And Diaz Break-Up Crushes Fans' Hearts.' That's sweet, but what compels me to read the article is a title like, 'Cruz And Diaz Break-Up Caused By STD?' That right there is what I want, Cameron."

He sat back in his chair. "Those headlines are BS, Jack. They bring up unconfirmed, unlikely things. Why do we need to be doing this when we are already publishing high quality journalism?"

"Our company is about blazing a trail, not following what other outlets do and have done. The Times is about innovating and changing journalism, and these headlines are going to be irresistible to readers."

Cameron shook his head.

"Listen." Jack took a hand off the table. "It's important that we do everything we can to continue a story, even if at first it seems like there is nothing else to it. It's clear we have a valuable asset that continues to increase each day, so we need to take advantage of it at every turn. I'm going to shop our site for some new advertising soon, and for what that will be, taking this approach with your headlines will make the next transition easier for you."

Cameron scratched his head. "I'll keep it in mind, Jack."

Jack pointed at him. "Don't forget Cameron, it's not what you've done in the past that matters, it's what you're doing right now."

He gathered up his team regularly to provide feedback for their individual performances. A few weeks later, Jack, Dustin, Cameron, and Jill all sat in the conference room.

Jack handed out a traffic report to everyone. "Listen up, I just want to let each of you know how great a job you've been doing since we started in January, but don't get too confident. We need to look at our existing content models and continue to evolve them each day. Now, let's take a look at how traffic is performing for each of you."

Jack looked up at his copy of the report. "Cameron, Mr. Journalism, you are our number one traffic producer. As we've already talked, I want to see you draw out stories, not end them. Your headlines must be more provocative."

Cameron put down the report. "I'm leading the company in traffic produced. Why can't that be enough? Why do I need to push a clearly unethical, shady means of reporting?"

Jack shook his head. "You still don't get it, do you? Journalism is heading in the direction of speculation, innuendo, and buzz. Hell, it has already started to go in that direction. It's not enough because that is not where the industry is going. Your writing needs to be for the future, not the present or past."

Cameron turned his head and didn't respond.

Jack tapped the table. "This isn't just for Cameron, it's for all of you. When you're talking about a Senate meeting and what came out of it, don't just explain what happened during it. Speculate on the future and the impact it could have in the coming weeks. If you're not creating buzz, you're not doing your job."

Cameron took a deep breath. "I'm not changing, Jack."

"You will, one way or the other." Jack turned to the next page of the report.

Jack looked at Dustin, but hesitated. "Dustin, you're the second highest producer of traffic after starting the first two months off at the bottom. I'm impressed with the way you've improved your content. You've generated some strong stories that have broken news before any other site. Some stories have been rumored and unconfirmed, but most have turned out to be true, making us look great. I enjoy the direction your content is headed in, even if some stories don't exactly pan out. Cameron, pay attention to what Dustin publishes, because you could learn a thing or two from him. Risks produce traffic. Keep it up, Dustin."

"Booyah. I knew you knew that I knew what time it was."

Jack stared at him.

"Strain, this is Dustin. Dustin calling Strain."

Jack put his head down. "Please stop talking; I literally have no idea what you're saying to me."

Dustin leaned back in his chair and pretended to zip his mouth shut.

Jack shook his head and looked away.

He turned to the next page of the report. "Karen, you've done adequate work, checking in at third overall in traffic. I would like to see more publishing out of you though. I know you try to do your best to find original news, but that's not the only thing that makes a great outlet. Original news is something we all want to report on, but the solid foundation of any successful website is covering the major stories that other sites cover. It might not be as exciting as original news, but we need those articles. Is that clear?"

Karen glanced back at Jack. "You know, we have a loyal audience and following because of the original reporting I've done. You should be grateful Cameron and I are trying to do honest, ethical work."

Jack slapped the table. "I'm begging you to think outside the box. It would do your work a lot of good. I can't hammer this point home enough. The old way of reporting is dead. We are defining a new method and you two need to contribute more to it."

Karen cracked her neck and looked away.

Jack looked at Jill and let out a sigh. "Jill, you are ninth overall in traffic for us. Ninth. We have interns and entry-level writers that produce more traffic than you. This isn't a job where you can fail miserably and still be employed. You're lucky I'm a nice guy, because if I weren't, I would have already fired you. Do you deserve this position or was it a mistake hiring you? This is your one and only warning. Bring in more traffic or find yourself another job."

Jill glared at him. "I understand where you're coming from, but you could be a bit more constructive with your feedback."

"I'll say exactly what I want to say, and you'll listen to it."

She looked through the report again to avoid eye contact with Jack.

Jack closed his folder. "Look, as a site we are doing a great job, but don't think for one second we can't get better. When you walk through that front door three words should be on your minds: traffic, traffic, traffic. I challenge each of you to find new ways to bring people to the site, and that means going outside of traditional content."

Everyone stood up, thanked Jack for his time, and walked back to their desks.

On his way back, Cameron stopped Jill. "Hey, I'm going downstairs to grab a cup of coffee, why don't you join me?"

Jill seemed distracted, but replied, "Okay."

Jill and Cameron walked out of the office, got into the elevator, and took it down to the lobby of the Infinity Building. They walked to the coffee shop that was across the street and got in line to order a drink.

Cameron took out his wallet. "Hey, don't worry about what Jack said. You're doing a great job. I read your stories and they're really good. It's exceptional work and Jack should know better than to ridicule you like that in front of the team."

Jill looked away from him. "Thanks for the sentiment, but he's right, Cameron. I'm ninth overall in traffic and the fact that interns are producing more views than I am is embarrassing. I'd fire me if I were Jack. What he said was fair and necessary."

Cameron paid for their drinks, and then they waited at the pickup window.

"Jill, he may have a point, but there's a right way and a wrong way to deal with people. Threatening to fire someone is no way to lead. Fear is not the way to motivate your employees. Sorry, but it's just not."

The two grabbed their drinks and Jill looked at him. "Relax, Cameron. I may be a woman, but I'm not weak. Besides, I need this job to work out for me in the worst way possible. Having been fired from two jobs already doesn't look good on a resume. I don't need a third."

They entered the building and got in the elevator. "You need to give yourself more credit, Jill. You're a human being, a great journalist, and you deserve a lot more respect regardless of job performance."

"It's easy to be bold when things are going your way, Cameron." The elevator doors opened and they walked into the office.

That day, Karen began to work on a story that had been broken by the Chicago Sun earlier in the day about a corrupt police chief. Knowing her job was on the line, she was able to craft a brilliant story about the Chicago police chief. It provided a unique take on the story and she was able to inject some alternative perspectives that no other site had expressed before. To her surprise, the story ended up claiming the top spot in traffic for the day.

Dustin's stories with unconfirmed facts and information were something he had become known for at The Times. The latest story that Dustin reported on was a rumor that Utah Senator Don Phillips, who was married, was having an affair with a 17 year-old girl. In the state of Utah, this constituted statutory rape. The information Dustin reported was not confirmed, but he published the article nonetheless. To the dismay of many, it was later confirmed that the story was all a rumor, so he made an update to his article. Dustin's story ended up receiving the most views for the entire week.

Jill took Jack's comments to heart, so she sat at her desk thinking about story ideas. She tried a new style of headline she dubbed: "What happens next" headlines. The story's title read: "Drunk Man Wields Flamethrower At Gas Station: You Won't Believe What Happened Next." When readers clicked on the story and saw the video, all it showed was a man getting arrested by the cops. Over the next month, Jill published stories like these and saw her traffic totals increase by more than 50%.

Cameron had the opportunity to stretch the truth in his headlines and articles, but he always felt the need to walk a straight line, never abusing his position as a journalist.

During a group meet at the end of August, Jack brought everyone together to review the totals once more. They entered the conference room and took their respective seats with Jack at the head of the table.

Jack passed out reports to each person. "As you can see, here are the traffic rankings: Cameron, you are first. Dustin, second. Jill, third. Karen, fifth."

Jill pumped her fist.

Jack adjusted his watch. "Nice job this month. We're now two places higher in national traffic. Remember though, we're only as good as our weakest link." He glared at Karen. "I'd like to start things off by saying, Jill, you have done a fantastic job. Your content has been gold, and I want more of it. Cameron, do you now see the power of headlines?"

Jill smiled from ear to ear.

Karen rolled her eyes. "Jack, are you serious? Those headlines are the worst. How can you possibly condone them, let alone encourage more? It's preposterous to think these are the types of things we need to be doing."

Jill's smile vanished. "Jealousy is a very powerful thing, Karen. My work is quantitatively better than yours. You don't have a leg to stand on here."

Cameron nodded. "Oh, please, I couldn't agree more with Karen. Jill, it's great you're getting traffic, but good lord, at what costs? Our reputation? Our credibility?"

Jack scratched his cheek. "Our reputation and credibility are solid. Readers are the judges of that and from the looks of things, they love what Jill is doing. Jill, keep it up. Karen and Cameron, maybe it's time to fully buy into this."

Dustin smiled. "Exactly. You two have the money, it's time to make the investment."

Karen looked at him, dumbfounded. "What? We're not buying anything."

"I mean you have the ability, Kare Bear. Look, we're on the Autobahn and there's no speed limit. Why not go 100 miles per hour?"

No one responded.

Jack took a deep breath and tried to shake off Dustin's comment. "Look, let's just stay on topic. I'll start with you, Karen. That was a nice article about the Chicago Police Chief, so why don't you do more of them? It's not illegal, nor is it a poor practice."

Karen sighed. "I'm an original reporter, Jack. You got what you wanted with that police chief story, didn't you?"

Jack shook his head and turned to Jill. "Moving on, let's talk about someone who is actually doing what I've asked. Jill, I clearly underestimated you. What you've done with headlines is nothing else if not innovative. That's the type of imagination and creativity I want to see from the rest of you. Step out onto an edge with your content, everyone, take it a step further. Sensationalize. Mesmerize."

Jack then took a long look at Dustin. "Do I even want to open up a conversation with you right now?" He paused for a moment. "Why the hell not? You've been rock solid reliable, but it looks like you're pretty happy being number two. I guess there's always a number two no matter what, it's the nature of rankings, but keep this one thing in mind, Dustin. Second place is the first loser."

Dustin laughed. "Say what you want, Jacky boy. I am one of the biggest content machines you've got. Go ahead and antagonize me all you want. I've got bulletproof skin and the best mind here. I'm not worried."

Jack shuffled some papers. "Cameron, you are still number one. You sir, are boring. It's always the same with you. The Greeks may have been a flourishing nation back in the day, but even their empire came tumbling down. That said, you are still number one in traffic. Good work." Jack leaned over to Cameron. "I can't wait until you're off the top, my man, then we'll really see what you're made of."

Before Cameron could respond, Jack stood up from his chair and walked to the front of the room.

He looked back at his team. "These first eight months have gone well, but keep in mind that what you think you've done well, you haven't even done on an average level. The high traffic you think you've produced doesn't ensure your job past this week. We are not a company that rests on its laurels. The Times is a relentless, unstoppable animal and I won't have any of you thinking differently. Stay on your toes, people, because one slip may have you falling to your termination." Jack clapped. "Keep up the great work."

By the end of the month, The Times had climbed its way up to the seventh place and was gaining momentum quickly.

Despite some of its less accurate work, readership continued to grow at a remarkable pace.

Chapter 3

A night after work, Dustin met one of his friends, Tim, for a drink at a downtown sports bar. They sat down at a high top and ordered a few drinks.

Dustin took a sip of beer. "Hey Timbo, what's good with you, brother?"

"You know me, D-man, same ole, same ole."

He looked at his drink. "Yep, that tastes real good."

Tim nodded. "So how's the big sis doing?"

"She's doing good. She and her husband Troy are in the baby cranking stage of life. They pulled the goalie and are in the offensive zone. You read me?"

He started laughing. "Like a book, homes," Tim said. "That's so cute, you're going to be an uncle. How precious."

Dustin glanced at the score of the baseball game they had on TV. "We all know I'm going to be the coolest uncle on earth.

I'm going to take their kid to the zoo and buy him all the candy, soda, and ice cream he can eat."

"And then Christina will kill you."

"Yeah, but I'm like a cat, baby. I've got nine lives."

Tim turned his head. "I guess you are a bit of a pus…"

Dustin laughed and pointed at him. "Watch it, meat. Watch it."

Tim took a sip of beer. "What makes you think she's going to have a boy anyway? What if she had a daughter?"

"Daughter?"

"Yeah, daughter."

Dustin looked away. "Then I'm sure I'll be the least relatable uncle on the planet."

Tim moved his glass. "So you glad you left the LA Native?"

"Oh yes I am. It was a cool operation they had going, but man, having to continue to write about the LA Marksmen was painful. Having covered that garbage baseball team as long as I did, I'm surprised I don't smell like crap."

"I mean, I wasn't going to say anything."

Dustin smiled. "Shut your face, now."

Tim laughed and shook his head.

"How's life at the bar man?"

"Business is good. People always need their booze, good times or not." Tim finished his beer. "How's your daughter? I haven't seen Kim in forever."

"She's good. I don't see her as much as I'd like to, but with Kim living with her mother in Newbury, it was a no brainer to take the job with The Times. Kim's gotten so big and is in middle school now. I can't leave her again, man, so I'm all in with The Times."

Dustin pulled out his pocket and showed him a picture of Kim.

"Aw, she's beautiful. Sure as hell didn't get her good looks from you."

They both laughed.

Tim flagged down the waitress. "Excuse me, honey, mind if I get another beer? Dustin, I'm assuming you want something with cranberry juice."

"Hey Tim, remember that time you walked in on your parents going at it?"

"Aw, dude, what the hell?"

Dustin looked at the waitress. "I'll have a beer."

She came back with their drinks and Tim winked at her.

"In your dreams, brother," Dustin said as he laughed.

"What?"

Dustin nodded at him. "Oh, you know what."

Tim looked back at the waitress as she stood by the bar. "I'll give that to you, but a man's gotta have dreams."

Dustin thought for a second. "Hey, man, so I was thinking about work, ethics, and all of that. It's sometimes hard to publish some of the stories my boss wants me to, so what would you do if you thought your ethics were in question?"

Tim leaned forward. "To me it's not a question. I look at work this way. Pick three things in life you will never compromise on, and be a total whore for everything else. If you can do this, you will lead a much less stressful life, I guarantee it."

Dustin checked his phone. "So what are the three you've chosen?"

"Money, fun, and entertainment."

"Could you be any more generic?"

Tim pulled out a story from his back pocket. "Dude, you never told me about this story you wrote for the Native. I found this while I was online yesterday and had to bring it with me."

He laughed. "I remember writing that. Can't believe people actually liked the story, even though it was a hell of a lot better than what happened in the game that day."

Tim read the story back to Dustin:

"It was another gorgeous day at the ballpark today, and quite possibly the best for the Marksmen yet. They lost today 10-1, but that's not what made the game memorable. This was the day the 'Chocolate Covered Everything' stand opened up. The most highly anticipated snack stand in Marksmen history was here and so were the fans. People showed up early for batting practice just to get a glimpse of Billy melting the chocolate bars into the steel pot. Slowly, the chocolate melted into a pool of brown wonder. You could smell the diabetes through the window of the stand."

Tim shook his head, smiling.

"Anticipation was high as the game's first pitch got closer and closer. In the background, some music about America played around one o'clock, followed by a smattering of boos at 1:30 p.m. About fifteen minutes later was when things really got loud. Cheesecake Bites were pulled out of the fridge. There was an enormous ovation from the crowd when the food was set down on the serving station. You could hear people getting fatter the more they gazed at the cheesecake bites. Sometime later in the game, we heard cheering but the bacon hadn't been brought out yet, so that was weird. We then kept hearing people say take me out to the ballgame, which was dumb because we were already there."

Dustin laughed.

"This was our moment, the whole game was on the line, and then Billy did it. He took out the bacon from the oven and lathered up piece after piece with chocolate. This was the Marksmen's closer and we knew it was game over. $75 worth of food and a few trips to the bathroom later, my stomach was filled. It was time to leave, and my originally white shirt looked like it had been buried in a County Fair Porta Potty."

Tim took a sip of beer.

"It was a truly historic day at the park with next to no one watching the game, 50 pounds of cheesecake consumed, and the equivalent of 20 pigs being purchased. This is Dustin Smith reporting, LA Native." Tim was still laughing when he finished reading the story.

Dustin bumped fists with him. "Thanks for the reminder, dude. Man, that story was fun to write." He looked at his watch. "Let's cash out, Tim. I've got an early morning tomorrow."

On Friday of the first week in October, it was a typical day with everyone arriving at 7 a.m. The site continued to climb the national traffic ranks, but prior to the end of the day, Jack called a company meeting.

Jack stood on stage. "We'd like to invite you all to a company party next weekend at the nightclub, Pur. This will help us all get to know each other better. The party is going to take place a week from today and will get underway at 9 p.m. I look forward to meeting more of you."

The rest of the day, the office was buzzing about the party, as people were excited to meet others within the company. Work was all but finished after the meeting and so Dustin, Jill, Karen, and Cameron all began talking about the party.

Cameron leaned back in his chair. "Hey, so this should be an interesting event, huh? Can't wait to see what the development team is like at a party. Things could get awkward, I'm afraid."

Dustin laughed. "Are you kidding? Dev knows how to party. Those people get wild and know how to have fun, or at least that's what Kaley from dev tells me."

Jill nodded. "Yep, it's no joke. I actually went out with Kaley one night during the first month we were open, and she drank Jack and I under the table."

Dustin, Cameron, and Karen all blurted out as one. "What?"

Karen turned her head. "Did you just say Jack? You mean, Jack Strain's my mind every time we have a meeting?"

Jill crossed her arms. "Yes, the Jack Strain you just disrespected. Kaley, Jack, and I went out with some other people from dev and it was a lot of fun. Something you guys don't know about Jack is he's actually a cool guy outside of the office."

Cameron spit up some beer after Jill's comment.

Dustin spoke up. "Honestly, I never thought I would hear the words cool and Jack in the same sentence. Ever. That guy goes with cool like bees go with water."

Karen started laughing, while Cameron looked around the office to make sure Jack wasn't nearby. He was on a phone call in his office.

Jill glared at Dustin. "What is it with you and your analogies Dustin?"

Dustin smiled. "What aren't they?"

Jill let out a small laugh. "Funny or entertaining."

Dustin looked at Cameron. "Well, that's mean, Jill," he let out a sarcastic weep.

Cameron got up from his seat and walked to the kitchen to grab a beer for each of them. They all cracked open a drink.

Karen glanced at the clock on her desk. "It'll be good to get to know you guys more. I think the party will be great."

Dustin stood up from his chair and held his beer in the air. "I'd like to make a toast."

Jill interrupted him by laughing.

Dustin looked at her with a smile. "You all right?"

Jill shook her head with a smirk on her face. "No, I'm good."

Dustin looked at each of them. "I'd like to make a toast to us. Fourscore and 10 months ago, our father, Eric Peterson, gave birth to a new outlet, conceived in tenacity, and dedicated to the proposition that we will kick our competition's asses. I see in each of you, the same jealousy that would take the wallet of me. I mean come on guys; can't we all just get along? How about this? Starting next Friday, we will all be known by a new name, none of this publishing team crap. Our name will be monumental, memorable, equestrial. I hereby dub me, each of thee, togetherly, The Four Horsemen."

Jill rolled her eyes. "Come on with that Horsemen crap. Karen and I are not men, nor are we horses."

Cameron glanced at Jill. "Obviously."

Dustin tossed his arms in the air. "It's a simple plural term. Horsemen. Your issue is not with me, it's with the English language."

The Times continued its steady climb toward the top of the national traffic rankings. The Friday of the party, 5 p.m. gradually came closer, and people began shutting things down. A few left work early to head home in preparation for the evening.

Jack was still in his office when Dustin went in to visit with him. Dustin knocked on his door and Jack waved him in. He took a seat in front of Jack's desk. "Jack, what clothes are you rockin' tonight?"

Jack put up his hand. "Wait, are we still in work mode or can we go off the record?"

"Uh, why does that matter? I'm just asking you what the attire for tonight will be."

Jack laughed. "Touché. Just so it's out there, we're off the record now. I think I'll probably wear a button down shirt and jeans. It's starting to get cold these days, so I may bring a jacket."

"You going to be bringing some crackers and cheese as well?"

Jack shook his head. "What?"

"I'm just saying you're boring, that's all. What kind of an outfit is that? Look, I'm not your mom and won't tell you how to dress, but from one single guy to another, you need to wear some PDs."

Jack hesitated. "PDs?"

Dustin sighed. "PDs, Jack? I thought you were better than this. So you know, PDs mean Panty Droppers, got it?"

"How old are you now? Five, six? You could have just said nice clothes and this conversation would actually be going somewhere."

Dustin smiled. "I could have, but where would be the fun in that? Look, I'm assuming you don't own any Rochelle clothes, right?"

"No, I do not. We're broke journalists. None of us do."

"Now, now, Jacky-poo, that's what credit cards are for. Look, I plan on looking amazing tonight and need to go there. You can tag along if you want."

Jack thought for a second. "Yeah, I guess that would work. We have another 30 minutes left in the day though. Let's finish up and then head over there after. Sound good?"

Dustin gave Jack two thumbs up and left his office.

Five o'clock came around, and Jack met Dustin in the lobby downstairs. They walked a few blocks to get on the downtown shuttle that took them to the Newbury Mall, which was the largest in the country.

Rochelle sold expensive men's clothes, and it was one of Dustin's worst vices in life. The two of them walked into the shop and began browsing.

"So what are you looking for, Jacky boy?"

Jack walked over to the shoes section and saw the prices. "$700? No way. Dustin, I can't afford this."

Dustin patted Jack on the back. "This is Rochelle, man. At this place, you invest in yourself. Besides, it's called a credit card."

"That's a good motto for life."

Dustin laughed. "Whatever you buy, Jack, just make sure it works."

"I can dress myself, Dustin. I am an adult."

"I see the clothes you wear to work each day. Blind people have better style."

Jack looked at a shirt. "I wonder what it would cost to keep you from talking for an entire day."

Dustin waved at Jack. "Oh, check it out, they have some items paired up. Let's see if we can't get one of these fine ladies to help us out. Excuse me, miss?"

The woman looked at Dustin with a smile. "How can I help you?"

Dustin pointed to the outfits. "Look, Papa Bueno already has what he needs. It's Papa Estupido who needs the assistance. We have a company party tonight and I'm trying to help Ugly, here, find something nice."

Jack rubbed his forehead. "Papa Bueno? I'm sorry, ma'am," he sighed. "Despite what this imbecile said, I am looking for something to wear, preferably affordable enough so I don't have to take out a mortgage."

The woman thought for a second. "I know exactly what you need. Stay here, babe, and I'll be right back."

Jack whispered to Dustin. "You hear that? She called me babe."

"Look at the time, the early bird special is almost over. Might want to get a move on, old-timer."

Jack stared at Dustin and didn't say anything.

The woman returned with an outfit for Jack to try on. He took it and went into the dressing room.

Dustin leaned over to her. "Hey, you really don't find that man to be attractive, do you?"

She shrugged her shoulders. "I mean, he has a certain confidence to him that I like. Why? Is he a jerk?"

Dustin laughed.

Wearing a dark blue collared shirt with matching slacks, Jack walked out of the dressing room and looked at himself in the mirror. "Oh yes, this will work."

Dustin hesitated. "Damn. You look good, Jack," he leaned over to the woman and whispered, "said no one ever." Dustin winked at her.

The woman took a step away from Dustin and looked at Jack. "It looks fabulous, sir. I'll ring you up."

Jack put his hand out. "Hey, wait a second. How much is this?"

She shook her head. "Price isn't the point, babe. Here at Rochelle, you can't put a price on looks."

"Oh, yes you can."

Dustin walked over to Jack and put his arm around him. "Give her your card, Jack," he motioned toward her. "Go on, give it to her."

She stepped toward him. "Ya, Jack, give me the card." She held out her hand. "Give it to me."

Jack leaned away from them. "You guys are like a slow motion roofie." He reluctantly handed over the card. "Just take it."

As the woman was walking toward the cash register, Dustin said, "Miss? Can you charge me for a pair of those shoes?"

She looked back at him. "Already did, doll."

"You did?"

She smiled. "Come on, Dustin. You know how we work. You don't choose the clothes, the clothes choose you."

Dustin looked up at the ceiling. "I love this place."

The woman came back with their bills. Dustin signed the receipt and gave it back to her.

Jack looked at the bill and his jaw dropped.

Dustin patted him on the back. "The price we pay to look the best."

Jack signed the bill and gave it back to the woman as he glared at Dustin.

That night at Pur, Dustin, Cameron, Jill, and Karen mingled with some Marketing people from The Times. The club was located at the bottom of an office building in downtown Newbury, with a bar at one end and a DJ at the other. A wide dance floor sat in the middle, with high-top tables sprinkled around it.

Jack walked over and patted Dustin on the back. "This guy. I love this guy."

Dustin looked at him. "Already at the bottom of the ocean, are we, Jack?"

Jack laughed. "I've had one drink. But really, this guy is responsible for why I look so good."

Cameron sipped his cocktail. "Who said you look good?"

Dustin and Karen laughed.

"Very funny, Cameron."

Chelsea from the marketing team came up to Jack and whispered, "Hey Jack, mind if I speak with you for a second?"

He nodded. "Sure thing."

They walked away from the group. "So listen, I got an update from Horizon on our current advertising situation."

"Is everything okay?"

"Yes, everything is fine, but they mentioned the next level advertising model you pitched to them. I think they're about ready to move forward on it."

Jack sipped his drink. "Interesting. Well, let's get some more serious talks going with them and go from there."

"Will do."

They returned to the group and Cameron pointed at him. "Hey Jack, so Dustin told me about your visit to Rochelle. Thoughts?"

"That money and time I can no longer get back," Jack said as he laughed.

Karen finished her drink. "It's good for ya. It's good for the soul."

Dustin looked at everyone. "Exactly. You've heard of Chicken Soup for the Soul, right? Well this is like Looking Damn Good For The Soul."

Karen turned her head. "You've done better, Dustin."

Jill pointed at both Chelsea and Jack. "Everything all right? What was that little chat you two had?"

Chelsea smiled. "Oh it was nothing. Just some work stuff."

Jack put his hand in his pocket. "Just thinking about things we can do differently, nothing major or worth sharing right now. Besides, let's keep work out of tonight. You'll all hear about this soon enough."

Chapter 4

During the beginning of December 2007, Karen arrived at the office at her normal time. Over the past few weeks, she had been boiling about some of the recent policies telecommunications company Horizon had implemented.

Karen put down her bag and walked into Jack's office. "Hey Jack, do you have a minute to talk?"

"Sure, Karen. Please take a seat."

Karen sat down. "I need to talk to you about an opinion piece I want to write."

Jack shuffled through some papers on his desk. "Sure thing. Who and what is the editorial about?"

"It's about Horizon and their bogus service policies."

He immediately put down the papers. "Horizon?"

She scooted forward in her chair. "Yes. Last night, I wrote up 1,000 words and have it ready to be published."

"Those words aren't the most flattering, are they?"

"No, they aren't, but I think readers are really going to love this. Their hidden fees and charges have cost people hundreds of dollars. I have documented proof of this and have had dozens of readers write in about this."

Jack folded his hands on the table. "Karen, you know they are an advertiser of ours, right?"

"Yes, I am aware."

"Do you know they are responsible for over 60% of our advertising revenue?"

Karen hesitated. "No, I didn't know that." She thought for a second. "I know they are a big advertiser for us, but this is something I need to publish and people need to hear."

"Okay, Karen. This is the only time I'll say this. We need their advertising and money. Be careful with what you say, because you will be held accountable."

"I know, Jack."

Karen published her editorial that afternoon and it garnered the most traffic of any story during the month of December. Not only did it receive major attention on site, but it set a firestorm of criticism upon Horizon that caused an exodus of subscribers.

Traffic was skyrocketing when Jack called her into his office. He looked at her. "Karen, please take a seat, we need to talk about the article you wrote today."

She took a seat in front of Jack's desk. "So, you liked it, did you?"

"I didn't like it. I loved it. This article is killing it in traffic and I just wanted to call you in to congratulate you on the editorial. Really, fantastic job, Karen."

Karen smiled. "Thanks, Jack. I was a bit nervous about publishing it, since it was about one of our advertisers."

"Horizon hasn't said anything and the traffic is great, so I'm happy."

She left his office and got back to work.

After 3 p.m. that day, Jack ended up getting a phone call. "The Times, this is Jack Strain."

He replied to the voice on the other line. "Are you sure?"

Jack listened to a reply and then said, "Yes, I understand."

He hung up the phone and called Karen back into his office.

Karen stood in the doorway and didn't say anything.

Jack sat quietly for a moment and then looked at her. "Karen, you're fired."

"What? Why? Earlier today, you said you loved the article."

"Things have changed. I'm sorry, but there isn't anything I can do."

She took a deep breath and her eyes wandered around the room. "Bullshit, Jack."

He sat back in his chair and didn't respond.

Karen looked at him. "Fine. But remember me when this place comes crumbling down. You just lost the only real journalist working in this house of garbage. Bad decision, Jack."

Jack sat back down and Karen stormed out of the room. "What an ass," she said to herself on the way out.

News of Karen's termination had not reached anyone in the company yet, but Dustin noticed she wasn't at her desk the rest of the day, which struck him as odd. Once he left the office, he gave Karen a call. She answered in a sad voice, "Hello."

"Hey, how are ya? We missed you the rest of the afternoon today. Is everything okay?"

"No, Jack fired me today."

Dustin paused for a moment. "What? That's unbelievable. Why?"

"I honestly don't know, Dustin. One second, I was in his office getting complimented on my Horizon editorial, and the next I was fired."

"Do you think this has anything to do with their reaction to it?"

"It must, because Jack said he loved what I wrote," Karen said and then began to cry.

Dustin replied, "Hey, come on now, you're going to be fine. Do you want to meet up and grab a drink tonight to talk?"

Karen sniffled. "Yeah, that would be great. Thanks, Dustin."

Dustin met Karen at a downtown Irish bar called McLoughlin's. He met Karen outside the bar. When Dustin saw her, he walked up and gave her a long, firm hug. "I'm so, so sorry."

"Thanks, Dustin," she sighed. "I need a drink."

The two of them walked into the bar, as Dustin's head barely fit under the low set ceilings. They sat down at a high top table toward the back of the pub. The waitress came over to take their drink order, and both of them ordered a double-shot of whiskey.

Dustin took her hand. "How are you holding up?"

"I'm hanging in there."

"So have you heard anything new since we spoke earlier today?"

Karen took a sip of her drink and nodded. "Yeah, I heard from HR. They are actually going to provide me with a three-month severance, which I find to be quite odd. I guess it's nice they're doing that, even though they still fired me."

He paused for a moment. "Huh, that is odd. I have never heard of a company doing that, but I guess that's something you can hang your hat on. Did they give any further insight as to why you were fired?"

Karen took a deep breath. "They said it was due to my inability to perform up to my compensation level. I did think, with the story I published today, it would go a long way in helping me regain a better standing with Jack and The Times. I shouldn't have written that editorial."

"Yeah, I hear you. I'm happy they at least gave you some reason as to why you were fired. Hopefully that'll help bring more closure to the situation for you."

Karen nodded. "Oh well, I think they are doing me a favor in the long run anyway."

"What do you mean?"

She finished her drink as the waitress arrived back to the table. She looked at the two of them. "Would you each like another round?"

Before Dustin could say anything, Karen pointed to her empty glass. "Yes we would, and two stouts as well."

"Slow down there, sailor, praying to the porcelain gods isn't *that* much fun."

Karen looked at him. "Please, it's not like I need to get up for work tomorrow."

They both laughed.

Dustin glanced momentarily at a TV. "So hold on, before we take this train any further, I still want you to answer my question. What did you mean by they are doing you a favor in the long run?"

"Look, Dustin. I took this job knowing the journalism profession I knew was long gone. I accepted this position because I needed it, not because I wanted it. My passion was gone when I lost my job at Global Insight and the publication closed. It was so disheartening to not only see that place close, but other outlets as well."

The waitress came back and dropped off the new round of drinks.

Dustin sipped his whiskey.

Karen tapped the table. "There are so many incredible journalists that now have to replace that income elsewhere, and how? Writing speculation, rumor, hearsay, and innuendo about people we've never met before? You can't even use the word journalism anymore. It's simply not what outlets are doing nowadays, and anyone who tries to do actual journalism gets lost among the garbage."

Dustin turned his head. "Don't you think you're being a bit harsh there? Sure it's a bit different from what the industry used to be, but there are still great writers out there."

Karen smiled. "Yes, I agree. They are writers, though, not journalists. Just because you own a website or can write for one, doesn't qualify you as a journalist. I know you love to cook, Dustin, but I'm sorry, you're not a professional chef. You're just not."

"Point taken."

"What's worse about all of this is that there are still institutions that uphold journalism for what it truly is, a public service. However, garbage sites just looking to get clicks only drown those people out."

He sipped his beer. "Sure, but people aren't idiots you know? They can tell what is BS and what isn't."

"They aren't? Then why do 24-hour news networks still exist?"

They both started laughing.

He smiled at her. "Okay, okay, you got me there. I have no response to that one."

She took a big sip of her beer. "My biggest issue with all of this is how it impacts people's perceptions. Perception is everything. If you can take enough quotes out of context and paint a picture of a politician in a certain way, what's stopping people from believing it? Supposedly, if you are a reliable source, what is stopping you from taking liberties with what you want and don't want to convey to people?"

Dustin put his hands up. "Now you're starting to talk about TV more than online or print."

She slapped the table. "No, I'm not. Writing institutions have the same impact on people, if not more. Think about it. Online news is so freely available these days. Anyone can go on the Internet with their phone and find information about anything. The ease of access is unprecedented, and the amount of users who are capable of finding information grows each day. If anything, this pertains more to online press than TV."

Dustin didn't have anything to respond with, so he just continued to drink.

Karen took another sip of her beer as the waitress arrived to ask if they wanted another drink. "Sorry to ramble on and on like this, Dustin. I know it's been a bit of a one-way conversation, but these are things I think about every day. I've actually been thinking this way since I took the job."

"No, don't apologize, Karen. I understand where you're coming from and especially can relate considering what happened to you today. I just look at journalism differently now. Sorry for using that word, but I just don't know what else to call it."

"Call it blogging."

"Okay, blogging. I believe the Internet has lowered the barrier for entry into our profession. I think that's ultimately a good thing. Blogging allows our industry to gain some brilliant, new thinkers that we would never have discovered without it."

She crossed her arms and sat back in the chair. "So that's what we should do as a profession, Dustin? Just whore out jobs to whoever has the ability to write about life? Journalism was so much better than that. The people who worked so hard to build up what used to be a respected industry deserve better. We shouldn't lower our standards just because we need to find a new business model. If anything, standards should be just as important, if not more. Being able to publish at a moment's notice is powerful, but if it's not handled with care, it can become a damaging weapon. More often than not, especially at The Times, it's the latter."

"Yeah, I know, but facts can always be added to an article. We can change a story with the snap of a finger."

"I think we have different journalistic priorities, which is fine. I definitely wouldn't have fit into The Times' long-term plans and probably would've just butted heads with Jack more and more."

They both finished up their third shot, and Karen took the last sip of her beer. The waitress came back and asked if they wanted any more drinks. Dustin shook his head. "No thanks, you can take this though," he said, handing over his credit card.

"You shouldn't have done that."

"Who lost their job again?"

She laughed. "That's sweet, thanks, Dustin."

The two of them got up from their seats and walked out of the bar. "So, what's next for Karen Drove? What are you going to pursue for your next job?"

She thought for a second. "That's a great question, but I know it won't be in journalism, writing, blogging or whatever you want to call it. I'm thinking I want to work in marketing."

"How dare you? That's like Batman going to work for the Joker. You're better than that," Dustin said with a smile on his face.

She laughed. "Hey, I know how journalism works. I know what makes you guys tick. I know what you want. Besides, I have ideas about where journalism is going and how marketing can take advantage of it."

"Interesting. I'm surprised you would want to go into marketing."

"I don't have to worry about violating the pillars of journalism there because I'm not a journalist anymore. I can let my imagination run wild."

"Okay then, Karen. I'll be sure to keep you on my radar, especially since you may be going into marketing now."

She bumped into him. "How did those words taste coming out of your mouth?"

"Know how your mouth tastes after you throw up?"

Karen smirked before giving Dustin a kiss on the cheek.

"All right, well, it was great to talk with you, Karen. Hopefully this helped get your mind off things for a bit. I'll definitely miss having you in the office. I will see you down the road."

"I have a feeling you will. Thanks for being so supportive."

The following Monday, Dustin walked into Jack's office first thing in the morning and shut the door. He took a seat in front of his desk with an intense look on his face.

"Hey Dustin, how are you doing today, my man? Everything okay?" Jack asked.

Dustin crossed his arms. "Fine, you?"

"I'm great. This past weekend I got the chance to go out to Pur again. Love that place. I actually met the owner when we had our company party. We're planning on golfing soon, he's paying." Jack winked at him. "When we go, you should come with us."

Dustin rolled his eyes. "Sorry, but if I'm doing anything with a long club and a small hole, I think I'll stay in my bedroom."

"Uh, gross. What is wrong with you?"

Dustin shifted in his seat. "Look, the reason why I came in here was I wanted to see what was up with Karen getting fired."

Jack paused for a second and looked at him. "It was something we had to do. I really had no choice. The type of content she produced, coupled with the fact that she wasn't producing as much traffic as we wanted, all meant she had to go."

"It just seemed so sudden, though. The article she published on Horizon was unbelievably good. Wasn't that enough to keep her around for a little while longer?"

Jack shook his head. "No, it wasn't. Even after she published that article, it wasn't even close to being enough to save her job. Again, the decision was based on the type of content she published and her lack of production."

Dustin sighed. "Man, that's brutal. Guess that means I need to stay on top of my game."

"Yes it does." He sipped some coffee. "So you know, we have some business that developed recently, and it'll help ensure a stronger, more consistent revenue stream. Dustin, you just need to make sure you continue to produce quality content. Keep bringing in that revenue in whatever way you can. You do that and you'll have a job."

Dustin looked at him. "What is this revenue stream, if you don't mind me peeking under your hood?"

"What about my hood?" Jack shook his head. "Not sure what that means, but as far as the new revenue stream is concerned, that's something I cannot disclose right now. We are trying to keep things quiet for the time being. Just know it's great for business, brings a new level of stability, and brightens our future as a company."

Dustin accepted Jack's response. He left the office and went back to his desk.

A week later, Dustin was sitting at his desk when he received an email from Karen that said, "Dustin, thank you so much again for talking with me the day I was fired from The Times. It meant the world to me and I'm not sure other people would have done the same. I wanted you to know that I found a new job as an Associate Marketing Director at Horizon. Thanks again for being such a great friend, and hopefully we'll work together again soon."

Chapter 5

Cameron sat at his desk one-day typing away on a story. The Times' traffic was now the fourth highest in the country.

As he was about to press "publish" on the story, his phone rang. "The Times, this is Cameron."

The voice on the other end was a company representative from the Newbury Stampede Basketball Club. "Hi, this is Rebecca. I'm calling in regards to the editorial written by Jack Strain earlier today. The piece is slanderous and we want it taken down."

Cameron's eyes wandered around his desk. "Where do you see this story?"

"Do you people even know who is running The Times?"

Cameron glanced up at the ceiling. "Please don't condescend, miss. Tell me where you saw this and I'll look into it."

"It's on the homepage. Make sure you do something about this or else there will be consequences for Jack and The Times."

Cameron went to The Times' homepage and found Jack's editorial.

"Newbury Stampede Owner's Alcohol Addiction Derailing Franchise."

Cameron looked up the Stampede's record. "Jeez, they're a .500 team, hardly a sign of a derailing franchise," he said to himself.

He then looked up the owner in the Newbury Police Department's database to see if there was any record of him having trouble with the law. "Nothing."

Cameron took a look at the site's current traffic analytics and saw the top article was Jack's editorial. "That's makes sense now."

He stood up from his desk, walked over to Jack's office, and knocked.

"Come in."

Cameron opened the door. "Hey, Jack, how's it going?"

"I'm fine, how are you?"

"Okay. Listen, I just received a phone call from the Newbury Stampede about your editorial. They are pretty pissed off."

Jack stopped writing and put down his pen. "And?"

"Aren't you going to take down the editorial? That thing is a flaming piece of garbage and you know it."

"Reallly? Well, I like to think of it as creative potential in action."

Cameron took a seat. "Okay, where is the booze? Have you been drinking?"

Jack laughed. "No, Cameron." He took a sip of water. "Seriously, Cameron, what do you want?"

"Seriously, I'm in here because of that editorial. You know the things you said are false. They are not that bad of a team to warrant a headline like that, and the Stampede's owner has had zero history of getting in trouble with the law."

"He is an alcoholic though."

"That's hearsay and speculation, Jack. If he is an alcoholic, no one knows about it."

"Exactly."

Cameron rolled his eyes. "What do you mean, Jack?"

"Cameron, when I want input from you about how to generate traffic, I'll ask. We needed more today so I took the lead."

"So that's our business plan? Using short-term, half-assed fixes to improve a below-average day?"

Jack slapped his desk. "You aren't getting it, Cameron. Among the people who have authority in this company, you are not in that group. Listen to me. You are on a string, my man, and that means when I pull, you move. You do exactly as I say without hesitation. Go ahead and push me further on this. I'm warning you for the last time, this is none of your business and it is out of your control."

Cameron took a deep breath and shook his head. He was about to respond but decided to leave.

Driving home that day, Cameron turned on the radio news to hear angry listeners and talk show hosts bashing The Times for the misleading editorial.

"It's outrageous that a company can get away with saying the things The Times said," a female caller said.

The radio host replied, "They are only hurting themselves with editorials like that. Their credibility will be damaged and readers won't trust them anymore."

Cameron turned off the radio. "That's what I think too. Jack has no idea."

While walking into The Infinity Building the next day, he noticed an article with a statement from the Stampede's owner. It was published in Newbury's local newspaper, The Metro. The headline on its front page read: "Stampede Owner Issues Statement Regarding Alcohol Use."

Cameron picked up a copy to find out what owner Mark Reynard had to say: "As a devout father and husband, I have not consumed one drop of alcohol since I first met my wife Tracy. Any reports to the contrary are completely false and untrue. We at the Newbury Stampede work extremely hard to put the best possible team on the court each day, and that will never change."

Cameron shook his head and put the paper back on the stand. He walked into the office and to his desk.

Before he could sit down Jack arrived. "Did you see the front page of The Metro today?"

Cameron took off his coat. "Unfortunately."

Jack smiled. "You see, Cameron? Creating news out of something that wasn't really news. These are the types of new opportunities and advantages we hold over an outdated outlet like The Metro."

"Yeah, Jack, that was really impressive," Cameron said in a sarcastic tone.

"Was that sarcasm?"

Cameron shook his head. "No, not at all."

"Just remember, Cameron, it's important to never be boastful or arrogant in this business. It can humble you just like that. Although, it's hard to deny, what I did yesterday was damn good."

Jack turned away, went back into his office, and shut the door.

Cameron sat down and said to himself, "What an idiot."

He turned on his laptop and then walked over to the kitchen to pour himself a cup of coffee.

As he finished pouring, Jill walked in. "What's up, Cameron?"

"Not much. What's going on with you?"

"Nothing, just excited to be here and ready to get the day started. It's a bummer though, sitting in here while it's 70 degrees and blue sky outside."

Cameron raised his eyebrows. "Yeah, the price we pay to be innovative and revolutionary." He took a sip of his coffee and walked back to his desk.

Jill followed him back and sat down. She turned around and looked at him. "What did you mean by innovative and revolutionary, Cameron?"

"Oh, sorry, I thought you understood what I meant. I was being sarcastic."

"I gathered that, but about what?"

Cameron tried to cool off his coffee. "Jack's editorial yesterday."

"What about it didn't you like?"

"It would be a lot quicker if I told you what I did like."

"Okay."

Cameron didn't say anything else.

"Hilarious, Cameron. You know that Jack's editorial is just a way to try and progress the business, right?"

"I think you mean regress. If we all started doing that, we'll be closed in a week."

Jill shook her head. "Not really. I published an editorial that rips on Rogue's new clothing line up. It's currently number one in traffic."

Cameron sighed. "What is wrong with people? Why do they read this crap?"

"Because it's entertaining, Cameron. Journalism isn't always about hard news, sometimes people need an escape."

"To where? Hell?"

Jill rolled her eyes and turned around. "You just wait, Cameron. You will see the light at the end of the tunnel. We all do eventually. The journalism you grew up with is dead and isn't coming back."

Earlier that morning, a plane crashed in Turkey and Cameron was the first one to cover it for The Times. A few minutes after he published the story, Jack asked him to come into his office.

Cameron walked in and took a seat.

Jack leaned forward in his chair. "I want you to cover that plane crash again, and this time, I want the headline to read, 'Plane Crash Could Mean Civil War In Turkey.' You need to do that before you go to lunch."

"What? Early reports are saying it was a malfunction in the plane's engine. There's nothing new that indicates this could possibly be the work of a rebel forces or that they even exist."

"There have been whispers, Cameron."

"Oh, come on, Jack. That sort of headline would be purely for the sake of traffic."

Jack smiled. "So do I need to say anything further then?"

Cameron shook his head and laughed.

"Look, Cameron, what we know is nothing, so until we know something, Civil War is the truth I want you to publish."

"With all due respect sir, that is the worst thing we could do right now. Our job is to find facts and tell the truth, not create false information and hope it turns out to be true."

Jack pointed at him. "Don't tell me what our job is. Your job is to generate traffic."

"Is that all that matters?"

Jack glared at Cameron. "For you? Right now? Yes. You do remember what happened to Karen, don't you?"

He nodded, walked out of Jack's office, and back to his desk where he began working on the story as instructed.

A few minutes later, Jack yelled across the office. "Cameron! Have you got that story published yet?"

"I'm working on it!" Cameron threw his hands in the air and then said to himself. "Jackass."

Cameron published the article and its headline read, "Plane Crash Kills Hundreds, Signs Of Rising Civil War?"

Once Cameron finished editing the article, he took a deep breath and published it.

He walked over to Jack's office. "This story is live now."

Jack refreshed his browser. "This is great stuff, Cameron. I know it's hard for you, but you're really coming along with what we're doing here."

Cameron stood in the doorway. "Jack, can we agree to never call what we are doing journalism? I understand what we need to do, but what we're publishing isn't journalism."

Jack thought for a moment and took a sip of his water. "Sure, Cameron, we can call it whatever you want."

Cameron's article grabbed the spot for most viewed article of the day.

Before The Times closed, Jack walked out of his office with his briefcase in one hand and two beers in the other.

After assembling his editors together, Jack said to the three of them. "Guys, I just want you to know we were one of the first to report today's plane crash in Turkey. While we didn't guess right with our civil war and death total claims, Cameron's article stole the day for us anyway. I'd like to make a toast."

He handed the beer to Cameron. "Here's to you, Cameron, for finally coming around and for just now beginning to realize your potential."

Cameron hesitated before clanking his beer against Jack's, and then he took a sip.

On his way home, Cameron called up his mentor Pastor Mike, whom he had met during college. "Hey Mike, how's it going?"

"Hey Cameron, it's nice to hear from you. I'm doing pretty well, how about yourself?"

Cameron stopped at a red light. "Do you have a minute to talk? I've got something on my mind and want to run it by you."

Mike replied, "Well sure, Cameron. I'm just sitting at home with the kids watching some TV. I've got all the time in the world, so shoot."

"At work, I've been having a hard time with our new business model and the things I'm being asked to do. It's all in such a gray area and I can't truly tell if what I'm doing is right or wrong."

"What does your gut tell you?"

The light turned green and Cameron kept driving. "It tells me I'm 100 percent wrong." He took a second to think. "But the old way of journalism is much harder and doesn't work with online media. Everything is so much easier and faster now."

"I think that's why they call it the hard way versus the easy way, Cameron."

"Yeah, but maybe journalism has changed, maybe it's not what it used to be. Perhaps, this new way is the best way, even though sometimes we get things wrong."

Mike scratched his head. "Aren't precision and accuracy the traits that made journalism so respected? To me anyway, that's what made it respectable and reliable."

Cameron shook his head. "Yeah, but can't this new age of journalism work?"

"Of course it can work, Cameron. I think the question you have to ask yourself is does it work for you? Can you honestly look in the mirror and be happy with the person staring back at you? Ask yourself that tonight."

Cameron adjusted his hand on the steering wheel. "I can answer those questions right now and I think the answers are both yes and yes. I just don't know how to feel about it though."

"That's something you're going to have to figure out on your own." Mike paused for a moment. "I would follow that up by saying don't compare yourself to other people. Don't worry about what other people think. Pray about this and see where God leads you."

"Hey, Mike, can I ask you something else?"

"Sorry, Cameron, I gotta run, buddy. It was great to talk with you," Mike said and then hung up.

When Cameron got home that night, he looked on his phone to see what the day's bible verse said. It was Mark 8:36, which he read aloud to himself. "And what do you benefit if you gain the world but lose your own soul?"

Chapter 6

It was now January 2008 and the beginning of the second year for The Times. The outlet had continued its massive growth and was now ranked second nationally in overall traffic. On a global level, The Times was now sitting firmly in the top five.

With The Times continuing its rise, they needed people to send to industry events to further the working relationship with colleagues. Every year, the Big Telecom Event happens and this year's show took place in Chicago.

Jack sat in his office thinking about whom he could send. "Cameron? Too serious. Dustin? Too Dustin. Jill? Jill, now she would be great for this," he said to himself.

The day before she left, Jack wanted to meet with her to make sure she visited some select advertisers who would be attending the show.

Jill walked into Jack's office, shut the door and took a seat.

Jack smiled at her. "So, Jill, are you all ready for your big trip?"

"Yes sir, I'm ready to go. Aside from covering the event and all that goes with it, anything specific you'd like me to do while I'm there?"

Jack folded his hands together. "Jill, here is a sheet for you." He slid it across the table. "On it is a list of five of our biggest advertisers. We would like you to stop by Terrence Computing, Mars Electronics, Horizon, Surface Comm, and Summit. We'll send a gift for you to pass along to each of the executives listed on the sheet. It's imperative they receive these, as this is one of the ways we ensure our partners know we go above and beyond to accommodate them."

"Understood, sir. Anything specific you'd like me to ask each of the executives I'll be meeting with?"

Jack nodded. "Yes, just make sure they are satisfied with the services we are providing, and see if there is anything we can do to help improve their advertising experience."

"Consider it done, sir. Thank you for this opportunity. I'll be sure to uphold our good name."

"I am sure you will." He cleared his throat. "You see, I evaluate the three of you quite often. Since you've been here you have excelled in this role, and I trust you above all else to represent us well. If you do represent us well, there is always plenty of incentive for you."

"Wow, thank you so much. I had no idea you were so thrilled with what I've been doing here. During my past jobs, the men above me have just been jealous and tried to supplant me."

Jack extended his hand. "Don't worry, I know about that. That was bad business and ethically wrong on their part. There isn't any common sense in mistreating someone because of his or her gender. My primary concern is to make sure people who help this company are rewarded for their efforts. That's the key to success."

"That's reassuring to hear, thank you."

It was Friday night when Jill had to get on her 6 p.m. flight to head to Chicago. Things for the Big Telecom Event began the next day at 10 a.m., so she had time to relax.

The show floor for the Big Telecom Event was enormous, and during the show, dozens of companies from all over the world piled into a massive space. Booths were set up for each company, all with their own theme.

Jill understood she had a reputation to maintain, not only for herself, but also The Times. The show began and she had appointments scheduled from 10 a.m. until 3:30 p.m., leaving her with two and a half hours to visit the companies listed on Jack's sheet.

Her first stop was at the Terrence Computing booth. She stepped up to the media relations desk to ask about seeing Howard Gardner, who was the company's Senior Vice President of Marketing.

The company representative on hand looked up from her computer. "Hi, I'm Jody, how can I help you?"

"Hi, I would like to see Mr. Gardner, please."

"Yes, and your name is?"

"My name is Jill Reddick from The Times. How are you doing this fine afternoon?"

Jody smiled. "I am fabulous, thank you for asking. Yes, I see your name here." She whispered to one of her colleagues.

Jill looked around. "Yeah, it's a great event, but I must say it's nice to get a break. Can't imagine how tired you all are at the end of the day."

"I love this stuff. So how was your flight in?"

"It was good. How was your weekend? Do anything fun?"

"Yeah, it was good. So did you experience any turbulence on your flight?"

Jill hesitated. "No. It was a good flight. Nothing crazy happened, just a normal flight. Did you take any vacation during the holidays?"

"Nope. So was it a big plane or a small plane?"

Before Jill could respond, Jody's colleague returned. "Mr. Gardner is ready to see you now."

Jill followed her to the back of the booth where she met Howard and took a seat. She reached into the bag she had with her and handed him one of the gifts. "A little gift from all of us at The Times."

Howard took the gift and opened it, "Wow! Thank you so much! What an unexpected surprise."

They both stood up and shook hands. Jill left and walked to visit Surface Comm. She arrived at the media relations booth to see Surface's Senior VP of Marketing.

Jill approached the booth. "I'm Jill Reddick with The Times. I'd like to see Barry Spencer, please."

Carol was typing on her computer when she noticed Jill. "Hi, I'm Carol. Oh yes, of course. Let me have one of my colleagues run and see if he is free." With a smile on her face, Carol continued, "So how was your flight?"

"It was good, no turbulence, and it was a big airplane. How is the show going for you? No stinky press, I hope."

"Nope. Did you have any delays with your flight?"

"No, it was on time. Are you going to any of the parties tonight?"

Carol looked up at Jill. "Yeah. Did you sit next to any crying babies or overweight people on the flight?"

Jill took a deep breath. "No. Do all of you have this strong of an interest in flights?"

Before Carol could answer, her colleague returned and asked Jill to come to the back. Jill walked into the room and shook hands with Barry. They both took their seats, and Jill passed the gift to Barry.

Barry's eyes lit up. "I never doubted The Times for a second."

Jill walked out of the booth and proceeded to make her way over to where Mars Electronics was located. Jill walked up to the media relations desk to see the head of Marketing for Mars.

"Hi, there, I'm Mary. How are you?"

"I'm doing well, thank you for asking. My name is Jill Reddick from The Times. I'm here to see Darren Clark."

"Certainly, let me have my partner in crime here run and see if he's available." Mary whispered to her colleague and then smiled at Jill. "So how was your flight?"

"It was perfect. We had zero delays, no turbulence, no crying babies or overweight people, and a massive airplane. Are you spending any extra time in town after the show is finished?"

"Nope. So did you find your bags all right when you got in yesterday? They didn't lose any of your bags, did they?"

Jill looked away shaking her head.

Mary continued to look at Jill with a smile. Her colleague returned and took Jill back to meet with Darren. As before, Jill handed him the gift.

Darren paused for a second with his hand over his mouth. "Well, my year was just made."

Jill left to go to the Summit booth, but couldn't get in to see them because of how busy they were. She did manage to receive a few positive words from the representative on hand and left the gift with her. "Hope you have a good flight home," the woman said to Jill.

All that was left was Horizon, so Jill walked over to their media relations booth. The representative on hand looked at Jill. "Hi there, my name is Brittany, how are you?"

"My name is Jill Reddick from The Times, and I'm here to see Mr. David Reid, CEO of Horizon."

"Yes, of course. Let's just see if he's ready first."

Another representative went to the back.

Jill thought for a second and then looked at her. "It has been a long day. Ready for a beer or two?"

"Ya. So how was your flight?"

Jill sighed. "The plane crashed and I'm the only survivor."

"That's neat. Did you recline your seat? I just love reclining my seat."

Jill bit her lip and looked around. The representative came back and took her into the conference room where David was waiting with a gift of his own.

David handed the gift to Jill. "Please make sure you give that to Jack when you go back to Newbury."

"I certainly will, David. Here's a gift on our behalf."

David looked at it and shook his head. "Incredible. Jack will certainly find our gift fitting, then."

Jill smiled. "That's great. So are you guys satisfied with the services you're getting from us?"

"Jill, we did have a problem or two along the way, but I can honestly say, right now, we are 100% satisfied with our partnership. Any time an issue has come up, we've had immediate access to the person in charge, and the problem has been dealt with in an efficient and effective manner. We love working with you all. Please let Jack know this."

"Wonderful. I'll be sure to pass along the nice words. It was nice speaking with you, David."

Before she could leave the room, he said with a smile, "I'm looking forward to more work from you all in the future."

She left and on her way out, waiting for her to leave was Karen. She had heard from a colleague that Jill was there to see David.

They gave each a friendly embrace.

"Hey Karen, it's so good to see you. I haven't seen or heard from you since you were let go. How are you?"

Karen had a bright smile on her face. "Yeah, it's great to see you too! I've been well, actually. I never thought I would enjoy marketing so much, but here I am. I must say though, it was always so hard to stay with The Times, especially with the direction the company was going. How have you been?"

"Wait, what do you mean with the direction the company was going?"

"Well, about a week after I was let go and had already joined up here with Horizon, Jack called me to explain the entire situation surrounding my termination. Horizon actually agreed with what I said and wanted me to come in and help change things, which I've done. Once he finished talking, I understood why he fired me and really, knowing what I know now, it's a good thing I don't work with you all anymore."

Jill stared back at Karen with her eyes squinting. "What did he tell you? What do you know?"

"Sorry, Jill. It's part of my job that I do not share confidential information, and what Jack told me was in the strictest of confidence. I can tell you though, I love journalism and will always love true journalism over anything else, but that's not what The Times is about."

"Huh, well, okay. I guess being honest with a friend is a lot to ask for these days."

Karen let out a brief laugh. "Friend? How many times did we ever hang out outside of work?"

Jill thought for a second.

"Exactly. Look, Jill, it's okay. We don't all have to be friends, that's not what good business is about."

"And you know what good business is?"

Karen looked at David who was nearby. "I'm beginning to, yeah."

Jill nodded. "Either way, it was good to see you, Karen."

"Good to see you, Jill."

Jill received an invite to attend a VIP party held by Horizon that night, but she wanted to avoid another awkward encounter with Karen, so she decided not to go.

The rest of the show went on as planned. Jill attended the appointments she needed to and flew back to Newbury late Thursday night. She arrived in the office first thing in the morning the next day.

Jill walked into Jack's office and took a seat with Horizon's gift in her lap.

Jack smiled. "Hey Jill, great to see you! How was the trip?"

"It was great, I delivered all of the packages, though Summit was too busy to see me, so I dropped it off with a rep at their booth. I hope that was okay."

"Oh, yes, of course, that's fine. Summit is Summit, you know. Thanks for doing that. So what was the highlight of the show?"

"Sleeping," Jill said as they both laughed. "I'm just kidding. The best part of the show was also the worst, in a way. I met with the CEO of Horizon, and wow, what an experience it was speaking with him."

Jack's face immediately changed to a serious gaze. "David is a good guy. What about that worst part?"

"Oh, well, I spoke with Karen at Horizon's booth and it was not pleasant. I'm glad she's gone."

Jack nodded. "It is good she's gone. David has told me about the great things she's doing there though."

"Oh, and actually Jack, Mr. Reid gave me a gift to pass along to you," Jill said while handing the package to him.

Jack opened it in his lap so only he could see. He peered inside and his eyes locked onto its contents. Jack smirked. "Great! Thanks so much for passing this along, Jill. I was expecting something in return from them."

"If you don't mind me asking, what did David give you?"

"I do mind," Jack answered.

A moment of silence fell over the room and Jack leaned forward in his chair. "Look, this is merely a need to know situation. That is the nature of business and what we do here. It's nothing personal. You understand, right?"

"Oh, yes, I apologize for prying. I hope you will forgive me."

"Forgiveness? There's nothing to forgive, Jill. Don't worry, you're my golden girl. I truly value your loyalty and commitment. I know how much you care, and that's what is important."

Jill smiled at him. "Thanks, that means a lot."

He stood up. "Unless there's anything else you need to report from the trip, that is all I need. Thanks for stopping by, Jill."

"No, that's it. Thank you so much for trusting me during the trip! It was an honor."

Jill got up and shook hands with Jack. She left the office, closed the door behind her, and returned to her desk.

Back in Jack's office, he received a text from Eric. "So, do you think she suspects anything?"

Jack replied, "No. I told you, she was the perfect hire for what we need. She's loyal to a fault and fears being fired more than anything else. Obviously we wouldn't fire her, but she doesn't know that. We own her."

Eric responded, "Yes. She is the perfect hire indeed."

Chapter 7

Over the next four years, The Times continued its dominance in traffic. In January 2012, The Times was number one in traffic on a national and global scale. No other website was within 50% of the total traffic The Times produced each month.

Jack was sitting in his office when he called Eric Peterson. "Do you have a minute to talk?"

"Sure, what's on your mind?"

Jack got up to shut the door to his office. "It's time for us to further our native advertising. My editors are in the right mindset to run with it."

"What do you have in mind? Our written form is pretty damn good."

Jack nodded. "It is. Brand messaging from us is strong, especially since most readers can't tell the difference between independent content and native content. That said, we can capitalize on this in a big way. We just need to find out what that way is. I'll speak with David and see what we can come up with."

"Do that and let me know if you need anything."

Jack hung up the phone and set an in-person meeting with Horizon CEO David Reid during the coming weekend. They met at Newbury Brewing Company, located in the cozy mountain town of Willow.

David and Jack met outside the brewery and shook hands, as they could see their breath in the cold air. "Hey, Jack, how are you doing tonight?"

"I'm doing great. What do you say we grab a beer?"

David patted him on the back and smiled. "That's the reason why I'm here."

The two of them walked inside and sat down at a table. They ordered a couple of beers and Jack cleared his throat. "I think we need to take more advantage of our native advertising situation. You pay us and we write great things about Horizon, that is all well and good, but we have ideas of how to evolve this model even further."

David took off his jacket. "In a moment, Jack. I first wanted to start the conversation off by saying how happy we have been with this partnership. Coverage has been more than exceptional in the native areas, and independent content on the site has been harmless."

"Yeah, and sorry again for the whole mix-up with Karen and her editorial. My editors now know never to do that to an existing partner again."

David shook his head. "That's okay, Jack. You handled it like a professional and it was never really a lasting problem for us."

"Speaking of Karen, why did you end up hiring her?"

David laughed. "You know that old saying? Keep your friends close and your enemies closer. I saw that editorial as a sign of frustration. When you let her go, I thought I would do her the favor of bringing her into an environment where she doesn't have archaic rules guilt tripping her left and right." He said, pointing to Jack. "I was a fan of her work and thought she would excel outside of journalism, and she has."

"So she's doing well at Horizon, then?"

"Oh, yes. She has a very liberated spirit about her and carries a potent enthusiasm into the office each day."

Jack was amazed. "Really?"

"When it came down to being on our side of native advertising, Karen has come up with some of the most creative ideas, after she helped us solve some internal problems."

"So, her editorial was right."

David leaned in and spoke softer, "Between you and me, yes."

"Well, I'm glad she has helped. I didn't expect her to be on the native advertising team though."

David glanced at the TV for a moment. "I had a talk with her about leaving her journalistic frame of mind behind. In marketing, you need a completely different mindset, which she has figured out."

David took a sip of his beer as they both sat silent for a moment. Glancing at the TV, they saw the Endless News

Network doing a profile piece on The Times and its rise to the number one most trafficked site in the world.

Jack looked back at David. "Now that's what I call a plan coming together."

"Cheers," David said as he raised his glass.

After a few moments of watching ENN's report, David said, "I have to give credit where credit is due, Jack. The Times is a force and your company is something we want to continue to support. Now back to what you may have been wanting to talk about, if you're ready?"

"More than."

"Well you know how we have native advertising in our current format, right?"

Jack nodded. "Yeah."

"Well, I'd like to take that concept one step further and make the same thing happen in video. What do you think?"

Jack looked at David. "That's exactly what I was thinking." He ate a couple pretzels. "What's your vision of it, in a perfect world?"

"It is going to be the type of content that completely engages the viewer. The media should be the type that goes 'behind the scenes' of our operations at Horizon and looks at different parts of the company. The pieces will talk about Horizon and all of the innovative progress our products have made. I'd like to see interviews with your editors and our executives, but in a way that is promotional. People won't know the difference."

Jack took a breath.

"The end result is favorable mind share with customers and, of course, bringing in more attention to The Times. This is something we can evolve and change as we go along. We will, of course, restructure our current contract to accommodate these new guidelines. Included in it will be monthly incentives and bonuses for hitting pre-determined engagement numbers. What do you think?"

Jack scratched his cheek. "This is very compelling. So who would make these videos? Who would create, conduct, and produce them? Who is reporting to whom? Most importantly, who is handling the cost associated with getting this initiative off of the ground?"

"First and foremost, I think splitting the cost and revenue down the middle between both companies is most conducive to productivity. That way, each company has the same amount to gain and lose. Agreed?"

"Agreed."

David sat back and draped an arm over his chair. "Great. As to the rest of your questions, Jack, we can hire a third party film crew to work with your editors to bring each feature to life. Having your editors on-camera will help the illusion be more convincing for viewers. We'll keep an eye on what's trending and then publish reactive content based off of it. Some of the more procedural and structural pieces we can get done now."

Jack shifted in his seat. "Yeah, that's fine. I'll be able to handle the types of reactive videos when we need them. Please don't hesitate to send over your ideas, David."

"I will, don't worry. In fact, reactive content is going to be the most important part of our native advertising. It's where we can really profit. We can send over some materials to help you get started. Anything else on your side?"

Jack thought for a second. "I do have one more question, David. How do we want to proceed with our new relationship from a public standpoint?"

"I think it's just business as usual, we don't need to be talking to people about our new initiative. You know what's revolutionary about an innovative idea?"

"What?"

"No else uses it, and no one knows about it. The Times and Horizon have an advantage over every other competitor, so let's not allow them to catch up with us any time soon."

"I agree."

David sipped his beer. "But in the event that people do find out, and it's probably only a matter of time before they do, just hit them with a blanket PR statement and that's it."

"Okay, I know exactly what to do. I'll be sure to brief our editors on this strategy. They'll want to know what's happening and how they can prepare for it."

The waitress came around for last call, so they ordered one more beer.

The waitress returned with their drinks. David took a sip. "So how do you think your editors are going to react to this? Are you worried about any of them reacting badly?"

Jack's eyes wandered as if they were looking for the answer. "Well, no, I'm confident both Jill and Dustin will adjust easily to this new concept, but I am slightly concerned about Cameron."

"Cameron? I thought he was your golden boy of news. Why wouldn't he want to get in front of the camera? Besides, if it's something he wants for his career, this is kind of the next step to becoming an TV anchor."

80

"Yeah, that's a great point. I'll keep that in mind for him, but let's see how he handles things first."

"I'm sure he'll be fine." David snapped his fingers. "Jack, so you know, there will be an eight second black screen that ends each video, followed by a small copyright disclaimer that also contains the phrase Sponsored by Horizon."

Jack nodded. "That's similar to the tiny disclaimer we have on written content. I like the eight second black screen because virtually no one is going to watch that, and if they do, they'll just assume it's corporate gibberish. People always miss the fine print."

David adjusted his glass. "Indeed they do."

Jack took a big sip of beer. "Right now we're definitely in a good position of power. It's where we want to be as a company, but with that said, we need to be vigilant and cognizant of the fact that some people may not like what we're doing. That's assuming our plan ends up getting reported in the wrong light."

"Agreed."

"At some point, people are going to find out about the native advertising, both written and video, so we need to do our best to be forthcoming about the concept before a competitor reveals it. If we're not the first ones to explain what's going on, we're going to be destroyed in the public eye, since our whole model is based around manipulating public perception."

David glanced at his watch and sighed. "Well I think that's it for me tonight. Time to head back to the hotel and then it's back to Paris tomorrow afternoon."

Jack stood up with him. "It was great to finally meet you in person, David. I feel like it's been long overdue, so it was fantastic to finally connect."

"It was great to meet you too, Jack. I'll be sure to have our lawyers draw up the paperwork and send it to Legal for review. Can't wait to get started on this."

Chapter 8

It was the morning of the first day that Jack Strain and his team would work on a plan to execute the video native advertising. Jack awoke at 6 a.m. and made his way into the office.

He and his editors began work on the videos at 7 a.m. With doughnuts and coffee on the conference room table, Jack, Cameron, Jill, and Dustin all took their seats.

Jack handed out the marketing concepts and ideas that Horizon had sent to them for reference. They spent four hours reading through the materials before they began to think of feature ideas.

They came up with the idea of having 12 videos that would be broad historical pieces about Horizon. Jack took a deep breath. "Okay, let's focus on segmenting the history of Horizon into a dozen videos. Deception and perception is key."

Cameron flipped through the marketing materials. "Why not just make one video of Horizon's history?"

Jack peeked at him. "We're not doing that because we have a content calendar to fill. Our coverage will have two parts that are crucial. The first part is historical and will serve as a building block for our Horizon coverage. The second part is going to be unscheduled and in your face, reactive videos. Topics for the latter will come along as they do, with no real schedule behind them. That's at least the perception I got from the conversation I had with David."

Dustin tapped the table with his finger. "So we are clear, Horizon will be telling us what topics to cover?"

Jack looked at Dustin. "Yes. When certain organizations or people do something stupid or have a fumble in the public relations realm, that'll be when we come in. We'll produce videos that will go live on the same day, exposing the target. Does that make a little more sense, Dustin?"

"A little more, but I'm still not entirely sure I'm picking up everything you're putting down."

Jack took a sip of coffee. "Okay, so remember when Global had the issue with a customer service representative calling someone 'a small brained cracker'?"

"Yes, cracker rings a bell."

"Well, if we were running this program at that time, we would've created a two or three minute video that day. It would have talked about Global's inability to satisfy consumers, alluding to Horizon's sterling customer service reputation. We would have promoted the feature all over our site and across our social channels. The same can be said for Horizon's outreach avenues. I assume more can change since we left the contract pretty open to what Horizon wants us to cover. How does that float your boat now, Dustin?"

"Leave my boat out of this. But yes, I got it now. Thanks for the clarity, J-Strain."

Jack cleared his throat. "Okay, let's get back to talking about the 12 history videos. Those are our priority right now. We won't have to worry about reactive content until we hear from Horizon or we see something worth covering on our own."

Cameron pointed to the packet in front of him. "How about we start with the company's formation?"

"See, I'm thinking that's at least two videos right there," Jill answered.

Dustin nodded. "I was thinking exactly the same thing. Love where your head's at, Jill. Keep it there, babe."

Jack glanced at Cameron. "Yeah, Cameron. Try and think of this as a way to dissect each aspect of the company from every standpoint possible. Horizon is an extremely large organization, with a history, so let's think of it like that."

Cameron raised his hand. "Oh, real quick, are we speaking about this publicly? How should we address outside concerns about this content?"

Jack produced a devious smile on his face. "Just tell them something, but don't tell them anything."

Dustin rubbed his eyes. "So for the first video, what do you say we get a few quotes from the founder of the company, Thomas Moreland? I know he's a tough guy to anchor down for a few words, but it would make our first video really pop if we obtained a few remarks from him."

Jill said, "That's a good thought. How about we do that for the first two? We can have the first one be about how Mr. Moreland came up with the idea for the company and end the video right before he decides to open it."

Jack clapped his hands together. "That's great. We do have access to everyone at Horizon, so do not worry about whom we can and cannot talk to. Jill, go ahead and put that feature on paper. Dustin, for the second video, structure that around the creation of the company and its first few months of existence. "

"Roger that," Dustin said.

Jack folded his hands together and looked at Cameron. "Now Cameron, go ahead and create a plan for the history of the company's first year. As I understand, it was a good year for growth. Summarize it and the events that transpired. Do not place any commentary spots in it because our fourth video will have reflections from people on the first year."

Cameron rolled his eyes. "Okay, but it will be hard to not make it the most boring thing in the world. I'll get it done though, Jack."

Jack pointed to himself. "As for me, I'll go ahead and create the bones for the fifth and sixth videos. No good feature series is worth anything unless you have a little bit of adversity. I'm going to spice up their first five years between the two videos and really crown them as a company that overcame enormous adversity. Who doesn't love an underdog, right?"

Cameron had a puzzled look on his face. "Jack, they were successful from the start. Why are you going to make it seem like they struggled? They never had any troubles."

Before anyone else could chime in, Dustin put his pen down. "Cam, I hear you, but trust Jack on this, and just worry about the videos you have to create."

"Fine."

The four of them crafted out the structure and process for how each video would be created. They all sent the forms to Horizon's marketing department for approval. David was the one who approved them and sent them back soon afterward.

"Okay, we've got them all approved and ready to go. We need to film and have Horizon edit these, oh, which reminds me of something. I spaced telling you all this, but each of you will be in front of the camera interviewing Horizon employees for the stories you have been assigned. I hope you all are comfortable with that," Jack said.

Jill smiled. "Oh, I love that idea! A little face time, why not?"

Dustin rocked in his chair. "Now you're talking, Strainey. I know I'll make that camera look good."

"Stop with the Strainey." Jack said.

Cameron put his hands up. "So let me get this straight. We're journalists, masquerading as journalists, creating paid, marketing-driven video content for a global telecommunications company. Is that right?"

Jack nodded at him but didn't say anything.

Cameron gazed out the window. "Sure, that makes perfect sense."

Jack rolled his eyes at Cameron. "Look, Cameron. The industry you grew up with has changed. It isn't what it used to be and you need to square with that. I thought you would've figured that out by now. Don't worry though, you will figure it out at some point. We all see the light eventually, it's just a matter of when."

They all got back to work.

Jack eventually broke the silence. "Okay, I think we've done some solid work for the first half of the day. Go ahead and take lunch, everyone, we'll meet back here in an hour to finish up the remaining six videos."

Dustin and Jill left the room.

Jack stood up before Cameron left. "Hey Cameron, want to grab some lunch with me?"

He thought for a moment. "Really?"

"Yeah, man. It'll give us a good chance to catch up a bit."

"That's fine with me."

Cameron and Jack left the conference room, while Jill and Dustin got lunch on their own. They walked across the street to the new deli store called Wich Paradise.

They ordered and picked up their sandwiches, then walked to an open table. After taking a bite of his sandwich, Jack said to Cameron, "Look, I know you're having a hard time with this native advertising business."

"I appreciate you acknowledging that, because this has been a weird time for me, and I can't believe it hasn't for Dustin or Jill."

"It's because they've accepted things and moved on."

Cameron took a sip of water. "Yeah, but they're journalists, they should have had a hard time with 'moving on', as you put it."

"You're not a journalist anymore, Cameron. That breed is dying, along with most print magazines and newspapers."

"I am a journalist, Jack."

Jack laughed. "Look, man, I used to be a lot like you when I was your age."

"Really? That's hard to believe."

"Easy with the condescension. I was like you until college, when a professor of mine changed my entire outlook on journalism, and life, really."

Cameron took a bite of his sandwich and then wiped his mouth. "Oh yeah? Mind telling me what happened?"

"Of course." Jack held his water glass. "I was a senior and it was spring semester. I was all ready to graduate and get out into the journalism world and make my mark on it."

"I think you've done that."

Jack put up a finger. "Just listen." He paused for a second. "One night I was walking around town just for the hell of it when I went past our school President's house, which was on campus. I don't know what it was that I saw, but I saw something inside that made me want to investigate further."

"What did you see when you did?"

"I saw the President of the university with a woman."

"His wife?"

Jack shook his head. "No, it was another woman."

"Oh, wow."

"Exactly. So I did what any curious journalist in my situation would've done. I took a few pictures of them doing their thing and then left."

"Too bad there wasn't the Internet back then, you could've gotten that story up sooner."

Jack smiled. "Ah, but given what happened next, it's good there was no Internet back then." He took a bite of his sandwich. "So I take a fleshed out, perfect story in to my professor, who also ran the school paper, the next morning. I had the photos with me and said, what do you think? We should publish this on the front page, right?"

"He said no?" Cameron said with a tone of disbelief.

"Not exactly. The President of the university had to have come by and convince him that it would be a bad idea to publish the story. I don't know how, but I always assumed that."

Cameron finished his sandwich. "You mean blackmail?"

"I don't know about that. Blackmail could have been the reason, but he never said why, specifically. What he did say was that we couldn't run the story and he had burned the photos."

"Are you kidding me?"

Jack shook his head. "Nope. I had given him the roll in addition to the photos and both were completely gone. There was nothing I could do about it. I felt helpless and deflated. Here was this man who I admired and looked up to and he just crushed me with a million pounds of disappointment all at once."

"So what did he tell you then?"

"He said to me, 'Jack, there comes a time in every man's life when they have to choose between keeping their job and losing it. That decision is always in your own hands, even if it doesn't seem like it. You can always control how you act, what you do and what you don't do.' That's all he said to me."

"That's bullshit though. The choice was between doing the right thing and doing the wrong thing."

Jack finished his sandwich. "When I was in college, I would've agreed with you, but knowing what I know now, I disagree. The world always seems black and white when you're young, man. I know, I've been there. But making decisions as if the world is black and white, when it isn't, is when you can find yourself in a world of trouble. Business is always shades of gray. There are always things that bother you. Things that make you want to pull your hair out and cry at the top of your lungs. What's telling are the people who can take it in stride and those who collapse under it."

Cameron sat and thought for a few moments. "I have never looked at work that way before."

The two finished their meals and walked back into The Infinity Building for the afternoon. Jack and Cameron arrived in the conference room a bit earlier than Dustin and Jill, so they did some work in the meantime. A few minutes later, everyone was in the room.

Jack scooted his chair closer to the table. "Good afternoon, everyone, I hope you are all ready to finish things up."

Dustin had an enormous smile on his face. "You bet I'm ready. Strain pain, just so you know, you missed out big time. I brought my lunch today. Turkey Club, honey wheat, honey mayo, honey bacon, honey tea. I call it five minutes of honey heaven. Oh yeah, and in heaven, there's a 5'8" blonde dressed in a honey bee bikini taking big bites out of my sandwich."

Jill rolled her eyes. "Oh God. I'm sure that's not the only thing that lasts five minutes for you, Dustin."

Dustin sat forward in his chair. "Relax, Ms. Vodka and Cranberry."

"Excuse me?" Jill said.

Dustin put his hands up. "Hey, don't rock the boat if you don't want to drown. Eating that sandwich really did feel like I was in honey heaven."

"God, please let me go to hell," Jack said.

Dustin looked back at him. "I'm thinkin' there's a good chance of that, Jackie-poo."

Cameron slapped his forehead. "Could we please? The obnoxious level in here is staggering. Mind if we act like professionals and get back to work?"

The three of them sat silently in surprise.

Jack looked at Cameron. "He's right. Let's get this thing rolling so we can all get out of here." He raised his pen. "If any of you need a refresher on conceptual themes or anything like that, materials are still in the center of the table for reference." Jack took a sip of the steaming coffee cup in front of him. "For the seventh video, Dustin, what do you think about creating something regarding how their customer service has evolved over time?"

"That really gets my gears turning. Do we have access to the previous versions of their customer service manuals or policies?"

"Yes, we do," Jack said.

"Brilliant! I'll get straight to work on that, Jackie baby."

Jack took a deep breath and shook his head at Dustin. Jack turned his attention to Jill. "Anyway, for the eighth video, Jill, I want you to cover the trial of Marston v. Horizon that happened back in 1995."

She raised her eyebrows. "Really? That wasn't exactly a good time for Horizon, especially from a public relations standpoint. Are you sure we even want to cover that?"

Jack scratched his head. "Yeah, I know Horizon didn't look good during that time, but my interest is in what happened at the end of the trial and what people's reactions were after it was thrown out."

"So is this a don't mess with Horizon kind of story? Or more of a spin on how honest and truthful the company is with its customers?"

Jack gave her a high-five. "Yes, that's exactly what I want."

"Which one?"

Jack put up two fingers. "The second one. Go ahead and put something on paper in the next hour or so."

"Okay, will do."

Jack turned his attention toward Cameron. "Video number nine time. Cam Bam, what would you like to do for it?"

Dustin put his hand up. "Hey, Strainey. Get your own thunder. You leave mine alone."

"As I was saying, Cameron." Jack glanced at Dustin. "What are you thinking for your feature?"

"How about a comparison? How competing companies' fees, hidden expenses and consumer distrust have all grown? This would be an investigative piece showing how consistent Horizon has been with their policies and how they've always presented consumers with transparency."

Jack pointed at him as he leaned back. "Now you're talking, Cameron."

Jill looked at the both of them. "Wait, doesn't Horizon have current plans that have hidden charges of their own? I mean, I'm all for this, but we don't want to shoot Horizon or ourselves in the foot."

Dustin turned his head to the side. "Don't be jealous, Jill, it's a good idea. Besides, Horizon's marketing department is able to reject any of our proposals, so we don't have anything to worry about that. Go on with it then, Cameron, shoot for the moon, big dog."

Cameron looked back at him. "Jack?"

Jack sighed. "I agree with Big Mouth McGee. Put something on paper and let's send it over. We will reconvene in an hour."

Over the course of the next hour, each of Jack's editors created the video plans they had been assigned. During this time, Jack answered any questions they had about their feature. When he wasn't answering questions, Jack sat at the table working silently.

An hour later, he put his pen down. "Okay, your hour is finished, where do each of you stand?"

"Finished," Jill said.

"Finished," Cameron said.

"Done and done," Dustin said.

Jack smiled. "Good. Send your proposals into Horizon for approval. Let's finish up the last three videos now."

Jack's three editors sent over their work as requested.

94

In the meantime, Jack was thinking and snapped his fingers. "Let's do three separate decade features."

Dustin lifted his eyebrows. "Come again?"

"Dustin, I want you to give a captivating profile on the first ten years of Horizon's history. Jill, I want you to do the same with the second decade, and Cameron, I want you to cover the third. All make sense?"

All three nodded and began to work on their features. After an hour had passed, they sent the final three proposals to Horizon's marketing team for approval. At the same time, they received approvals from Horizon for the seventh, eighth and ninth videos.

Jack smiled. "All the videos have been approved."

Cameron put his hand on the table. "Wait, seriously? They accepted the proposal I sent in for my feature?"

Jack took a look at the email again. "Yes, they did, and I am quoting their email here. 'All three videos have been accepted. On a side note, we love the proposal Cameron sent in. The angle he's taking with that story is perfect.' Good job, Cameron."

"Wow, thanks for passing along their note, Jack. I didn't know I was so on point. Good to know for future reference."

Jill scratched her forehead. "Yeah, that is surprising, but good for you, Cameron. It's great to see you coming around with this stuff. I thought you were never going to really get it."

"Same here, but I did have a pretty powerful talk with Jack at lunch. He gave me some great insight into how he's looking at all this. I appreciate that again, Jack."

He nodded.

"Jack?" Jill said.

"Insightful? I mean come on, if anyone in this room is, it's me. Just call me Buddha." Dustin said.

Jack said with a proud look on his face. "No sweat, Cameron, I know you're a good guy and your heart is in the right place. You just needed someone to relate to you."

Dustin scratched his cheek. "Wow."

Jack collected the papers in front of him and placed them into a nearby folder. "As far as I'm concerned, everyone, we're done with things on our side, so I think we deserve a celebratory beer. Hey Booooouda, do you mind grabbing each of us a beer?"

"Cute. No, I don't mind at all." Dustin went to the kitchen and then passed out a beer to each of them when he returned.

Cameron took a sip of his beer. "So what do you see our reactive content looking like?"

Jack winced. "That's tough to say because reactive means something has happened and Horizon needs immediate spin coverage from us. Since we haven't seen any examples of what they'd like spun, it's hard to say. All I can tell you at this point is be ready, creative, and open-minded when things do come up."

It was now close to 7 p.m. and they were the only ones left in The Times' office. While they were waiting to hear back on the last three videos, Jack decided to pull up their editorial calendar. "While we wait, why don't we go ahead and date our history features for the year."

Jill took a sip of beer. "We know the order of which videos will go live first, but when do we want to start scheduling them? Don't we need to set filming dates first?"

Jack was still looking at the editorial calendar in front of him. "Yes, those will commence later this month, so no need to worry about that. We will begin publishing our features on April 1st. Let's schedule from our second feature to our 12th."

Cameron raised his hand. "We need to set 11 more up for publishing over the next eight months, so why don't we just space them out every three weeks."

Jack nodded. "Okay, done. Oh, it looks like Horizon has approved our final three videos. There's also a message from David Reid, so hang on one second while I read it."

Shocked and caught off guard by what David sent him, Jack looked up at his team. "It looks like Horizon is sending a film crew here tomorrow as they want us to begin producing reactive content right away. I want everyone here at 7 a.m."

Cameron put his hand up. "Wait a second Jack, I think you and Horizon are forgetting something. None of us have any experience being on-camera, let alone knowing what reactive content is anyway. I thought we were going to have more time to prepare."

Jack looked at Cameron. "I hear you and this is all less than ideal, but we still need to make things happen. This is why I said earlier, be ready, creative, and open-minded. I hope we can do that tomorrow. Let's not allow excuses to get in our way."

"Can do," Cameron said as he finished his beer.

"I'm a certified stud in whatever I do, so don't worry, Jack. I'll be here ready to rock bright and early, baby," Dustin said as he finished his beer and slammed it on the table.

"Please don't call me baby."

"Baby isn't bad compared to some other nicknames I could send your way."

Jill slapped her forehead. "Shut it, Dustin. Jack, don't worry, we'll all be prepared. You have nothing to worry about."

Dustin made a sniffing sound.

Jill rolled her eyes. "What, Dustin?"

"Nothing, thought for a moment I smelled poo when you spoke."

"Dustin!" Jill said.

Jack stood up. "We're done here. Everyone has what they need. Be here at 7 a.m. Good night."

Chapter 9

"Reports are coming out of Los Angeles that telecommunications giant, Revision Communications, is about to be involved in a class-action lawsuit, in which consumers are suing the corporation for purposefully limiting Internet connections. Revision allegedly capped the performance of its low-end connection speed, below what was advertised, without informing its customers, in turn forcing many to pay a higher rate for its faster connection speed. The difference between the two connection speeds in monthly price is roughly $60. We reached out to Revision Communications for an official statement, but they declined to comment at this time," ENN anchor, Jamie Carol, said.

Dustin turned off his TV and got into his car to drive to work. "Revision is a bunch of morons if that story turns out to be true," He thought to himself.

Dustin arrived downtown at 6:45 a.m., went to buy himself some tea, and then took the building's elevator up to The Times' floor. He walked inside and went straight to Jack's office. "Tell me what time it is, Jacky."

"It's 6:56 in the morning," Jack said.

"No, tell me what time it is, you know?"

"You can't do this to me this early in the morning, Dustin. What do you want?"

Dustin stood while he put his hands on the chair in front of Jack's desk. "Did you hear about the situation with Revision?"

"Wouldn't it have been easier to just start off with that?"

"Still waiting on the time, J-Strain."

Jack didn't reply and stared at him.

"It's game time, baby, come on Jacky. You should've known that."

Jack tilted his head back. "Why don't you just…forget about it? I did hear about the Revision story, and we'll be covering that today. See you all in the conference room in 10 minutes. Make sure you tell the other two to be there."

"Roger that."

Jack rolled his eyes as he left the room.

Dustin set down his briefcase and took a sip of his tea. Both Cameron and Jill were already at their desks preparing for the day.

"Jill and Cameron, conference room in 10 minutes," Dustin said.

"Got it," Cameron said.

"Will do," Jill said.

They all walked into the conference room together followed by Jack, who sat down and turned the TV on. He changed the channel to ENN where the Revision story was still being discussed. "Everyone, this is our first crack at reactive content. We are going to bury these clowns in this, all the while promoting Horizon. Let's begin brainstorming for today's video, shall we?"

Dustin tapped his chin. "Well, the way I'm reading this, it's simple."

Jack put out his hand. "Do tell."

"First, let's elaborate and really dwell on how Revision's shady business tactic has severely damaged consumer trust. I emailed Karen this morning, and she said former Revision customers are already jumping ship to Horizon. We can take that and accentuate the fact that people are switching to the better, more consumer friendly organization, Horizon. And finally, let's highlight how Horizon's Internet speeds are faster and cheaper than those of Revision's."

"I like the sound of that, Dustin," Jill added.

Cameron rubbed his eyes. "So who at Horizon do we want to interview for this feature?"

Jack looked at his email to check something. "It looks like Horizon has already flown in their director of product development and their senior vice president of marketing. David says they should arrive here in an hour. The film crew will be here in fifteen minutes."

Dustin put up his hand. "Whoa, whoa, Strainey baby, you can't rush this," he said pointing to his face. "This takes time. A great performance for Babe Ruth took nine innings, not an hour or 15 minutes. Let me marinate for a while, get some flavor, and then I'll be ready to grill."

Jack sighed. "I'm this close to quitting."

"Well, now go, walk out the door. Just turn around now. 'Cause you're not welcome anymore."

"Please, God, take me now," Jack said as he looked at the ceiling. "Without saying another word, Dustin, create a plan for how the feature will run. Do it within the guidelines of us first interviewing the director of product development and then finishing up with Revision's marketing SVP."

"Lovin' it, baby Strain," Dustin said as he began to work.

Fifteen minutes later Dustin looked up. "The plan is a go for launch."

"Great. It looks like the film crew has just arrived. I want everyone to head over to go see their stylist and get some makeup done," Jack said.

"Makeup? On this face, Jacky? You wouldn't Photoshop the Mona Lisa, would you?"

"No, Dustin, but you might as well be the Mona Ugly, so make sure you get some makeup done before you start shooting."

Jill shook her head. "Stop being such a drama queen, Dustin. Come on guys, let's get moving."

Jill, Cameron, and Dustin all walked over to the stylist. When they were finished, Jerry Zaun, who was the director of product development, and Nikki Kane, who was the senior vice president of marketing, both walked into the office.

"Jerry! Nikki! Great to finally meet you two," Jack yelled across the room.

They walked over and shook Jack's hand.

"Very nice to meet you too, Jack," Nikki said.

"It's a pleasure," Jerry said.

Jack smiled. "So how were the flights getting into Newbury? I hope everything went smoothly and getting to our office wasn't a problem."

Nikki shook her head. "No, everything went perfectly, and we're here on time. What more could we ask for?"

"Some dynamite reactive content is what you could ask for and it's what you're going to get," Jack said as he pointed at her.

"Okay, so shall we get started?" Jerry said.

Jack rubbed his hands together. "Absolutely! Dustin, let's have you start off the segment interviewing Jerry, like your plan says. Jill, looks like you will then interview Nikki; and Cameron, you will wrap everything up and give us a sexy conclusion. All good?"

Dustin walked in front of him. "Better go find a helmet, Jack, because I'm about to blow your mind."

A green screen was set up by the film crew and served as the location for where the interviews would be done.

Cameron had a surprised look on his face. "Hey Jack, what's with the green screen?"

"Oh that? In post-production, they will project some floating screenshots of Horizon's headquarters and some general thematic images. There's nothing to worry about. It'll all look good."

"If you say so."

The set was ready and Jack located the first two people. "Dustin and Jerry, you two are up now."

Both of them walked onto the set and took their seats, one facing the other.

Jerry leaned over to Dustin. "Okay, so what do you want to start with?"

"Well, seeing as I've never done this before, I'd just say follow my lead, and we'll tip-toe our way through this. I may make a mistake or two, so hang with me and don't be afraid to laugh."

"Okay."

Dustin looked up at the people behind the set. "Anyone want to give us a countdown?"

Jack stood up from his chair. "Rolling in three, two, one, action!"

"So who are you and what do you do at Horizon?" Dustin said.

"My name is Jerry Zaun and I am Horizon's director of product development."

"Tell us a little bit about what you do each day."

Jack walked in front of the camera. "Cut, cut, cut. Hey, Dustin? This isn't show and tell at kindergarten, okay? Get to the point already. This is only a six or seven minute feature."

"Do you have a better suggestion? I'm all ears, Mr. Sporsese."

Jack put his hands on his hips. "Should I even ask?"

"Scorsese and Spielberg. I mean come on, tell me those two as one person wouldn't just be epic. I mean come on, come on, Jacky."

"Focus, Dustin!" Jack said as he pointed at him. "Talk about what happened with Revision today and then transition into Horizon's products and offerings."

"Got it."

Jack walked behind the camera. "Rolling in three, two, one, action!"

"As I'm sure you heard today, Revision Communications has been caught up in a class-action lawsuit for false advertising. What is your reaction to this news, Jerry?" Dustin said.

"Well, Revision is supposed to be a first-class company and as someone who works on Horizon's product side, I don't know how they could've missed this. The only logical conclusion is it was done on purpose. When we build a product for our consumers, we make sure it delivers the best service at the best price."

Dustin peeked down at his notes. "How does the company decide on the price people pay for the connection speed they end up getting?"

"While I can't speak to the exact prices themselves, we make sure our lower-end speed is 20% faster than our competition's. It's part of the competitive edge we hold over other companies, and I think people who currently subscribe with us would agree."

"So where's the disconnect then? It's seems obvious that a company wouldn't want to cheat its customers when they know the truth will eventually get out, yet Revision still did. What motivates that sort of decision-making?"

Jerry shifted in his seat. "It's difficult to know for sure. Horizon is not that type of company, and I would never work for a company that treated its customers in such a manner."

"Well, there you have it. We'll be right back to discuss things further with Horizon's senior vice president of marketing, Nikki Kane."

Jack interrupted things again. "Dustin, one more time, please. Eliminate the 'well there you have it' comment."

"I feel like you're whining about a drop of water missing from the ocean."

"Just do it."

"We'll be right back to discuss things further with Horizon's senior vice president of marketing, Nikki Kane."

The cameras stopped, and the two walked off the set. As they stood behind the camera, Jill and Nikki took their seats across from each other.

Jack approached the two of them. "Jill, do you know where to start with this?"

"Not really, no, but I'm going to get it done anyway."

Jack took a step back and looked to see where everyone in the room was. "Good. Cameron, make sure you're paying close attention, because I'm counting on you to wrap all of this up into a nice conclusion. Let's get this thing rolling. Three, two, one, action!"

"Hello, and welcome back. We are here with Ms. Nikki Kane, Horizon's senior vice president of marketing. Welcome, Nikki."

"Thank you, Jill. It's a pleasure to be joining you today."

"So we've discussed the product side and some of the theory that may have gone into Revision's thinking, but it's clear the strategies and business models Horizon has implemented are working very well."

"Our outstanding customer service is part of why you see so many Revision customers leaving their current subscriptions and coming over to Horizon."

"How many people have switched and why?"

"Well, we've seen a significant increase in new subscribers already today. A lot of the feedback they're sending us is about the class-action lawsuit. Horizon is a consumer first company and we value consumer trust more than anything else. Our Internet speeds are faster than Revision's. Not only that, but our prices are far more affordable."

"Those are just words. What numbers can you provide to help support your comments?"

Jack eyes were wide open. "Cut, cut. Easy, Jill. We're working with Horizon, not against them."

"I know that. I didn't think I was being too direct, was I, Nikki?"

"No, I actually thought what you said was fine."

Jill looked back at him. "Jack?"

"Look, if you're really fine with it, Nikki, then don't mind me."

"I'm fine with it."

"Then let's keep rolling."

Jill turned back to Nikki. "What quantitative support can you provide to help back up those statements?"

"Our low-end Internet speed is 20% faster than Revision's. Not only that, but the price we offer is $5 less per month. We offer superior services at a market-winning price. Those who have not yet made the jump to Horizon should now see pretty clearly that we are the best option around."

"Those are significant numbers and are impossible to ignore. I'll sure be switching services when I get home tonight." Jill laughingly said.

Nikki laughed with her. "Hey, why don't I help you get started right now?"

"Great idea, Nikki," She paused. "What about hidden expenses, people always worry about those cropping up. How does Horizon handle those?"

"We have none, plain and simple. Our mission is about being open and honest with people, while providing professional services at affordable prices. Horizon is the future and we'll only continue to evolve our products to best serve consumers."

"Thank you for the time, Nikki. We'll be right back."

Jack jumped with excitement. "And cut! Brilliant stuff, ladies, thanks so much."

The two of them left the set and walked into the kitchen to pour themselves some coffee.

Meanwhile, Cameron finished writing some notes for what he wanted to say.

Jack clapped. "Cameron, are you ready to end this sucker in style?"

"Yes, I'm ready to go."

Cameron walked onto the set but didn't sit down. He stood up for the final video.

Jack raised an eyebrow. "Cameron, aren't you going to take a seat? Everyone else has done that."

"Yes, everyone else has done that, but they all also had someone to talk with. I'm not interviewing anyone, so I think this will come across much better if I'm standing. It'll feel more organic."

"Let's see what you got. Rolling in three, two, one action!"

Cameron stepped forward and looked directly into the camera. "From everything you've heard today, there are two very clear takeaways regarding Revision Communications and Horizon. On one hand, you have Revision, a company that has a large market share. They've abused their position of power and isn't that really the test of a company? When an organization has the superior edge in the marketplace, what do they try to do with this advantage? Do they run with a good thing and continue to provide quality services at a fair price or do they decrease service while keeping prices high? It's pretty clear which choice Revision has made, and now consumers are the ones paying for it, in more ways than one."

He paused for a second.

"Despite the astonishing shortcomings of a company people once trusted, don't worry, because there is a solution. There is a beacon of hope on the Horizon. It's worth noting that it can sometimes be difficult to sort the truth from falsehood. No matter what though, you can always count on The Times."

Jack smiled from ear to ear. "Yes, Cameron, that's what I'm talking about." He pumped his fist in the air and walked over to give Cameron a high five.

Dustin walked up to Cameron to give him a handshake congratulating him on finishing up the video.

Jill patted him on the back. "Cameron, I have to admit, that wasn't an easy thing to do. I have newfound respect for you, my friend."

"Thanks. It just felt right and was easy to execute. I thought everyone did great today."

Jack smiled. "Yes, absolutely. Everyone did fantastic work today, but now it's time to get this out into the public eye. We're not done working yet."

They thanked Nikki and Jerry for the time, and then the two left with the film crew shortly after.

A few hours later, Jack and his team met in the conference room to review the final cut of the video.

Everyone sat down and Jack put his hands on the table. "Let's take a look at the video and see what we think. Make sure each of you are paying close attention to yourselves on screen. I want to see improvements the next time we film. Yes, you three did a fine job, but it can and needs to be better, no matter what." Jack played the clip and they all watched with anticipation.

The video played through one time with the music, themes, and presentation all complete.

"Wow," Dustin said.

"Okay," Cameron said.

"Huh," Jill said.

Jack looked at each of them. "Anyone else care to give more than one word's thought on our first freakin' video?"

Dustin paused. "I think when you consider the job that each of us did, things are heading in the right direction. The music is certainly questionable, though, Jack."

Jill laughed. "It's almost like the video is a cheesy paid programming ad with that music."

Cameron leaned forward in his chair. "But it's just the music, not us. I think the camera angles, Horizon office cutscenes, and backgrounds are all perfect. But really, the music needs to go. Who put that in there, Jack?"

Jack hesitated. "It, uh, was not Reach Media."

Jill turned her head to the side. "What? Weren't they the ones adding music?"

"I decided to add in that music. I know one of the editors at Reach and he helped me out," Jack said with a tone of guilt.

All three of them burst out laughing.

"Ouch, Jack. That's your taste in music?" Cameron said.

"So you know, Jack, it tastes bad," Dustin said.

Jack slapped the table. "Well, what did you expect? I had to have some hand in this. I wasn't going to stand by and do nothing."

Jill smiled as she tried to hold back further laughter. "We admire that, Jack, but why don't you just make an appearance in our next video? I mean the music side of you is clearly not in line with this video."

Jack turned his head. "Okay, I'll get in on the next one."

She adjusted her hair. "So where do we go from here?"

"I'll go ahead and send some feedback to Reach Media and tell them to put in better background music," Jack said. He sent the email and then awaited a response from Reach Media. 30 minutes later he heard back, and they sent a completely revised version for review.

Jack played it and all four of them agreed it was ready for publishing.

The Times published the feature to the millions of people who followed them on social media, while Horizon played it through their On Demand service and other channels. Every major news network in the country picked up the Times' video.

Dustin left the office and drove over to his older sister's house for dinner. He rang the doorbell, and the front door swung open with his smiling sister Christina standing there. "Little bro!"

Smiling back at her, Dustin replied, "Hey, Christina, how are you doing?"

They hugged each other and Dustin walked into the house where Christina's husband, Troy, greeted him. "Hey, Dustin, great to see you man."

"Great to see you too."

Dustin shook hands with him, and the three of them walked into the living room where Troy and Christina's one year-old son, Max, was sleeping.

Dustin leaned over the crib. "How's the big fella doing?"

Christina put her arm around Troy. "He's good. We finally put him down for a nap about 10 minutes ago, so now we can have ourselves a little adult time."

"I bet you guys need adult time whenever you can get it. I can't imagine having a child right now."

Christina laughed. "I can't either."

"Hey, don't be like that, Christina. He's your brother, after all. Don't worry, Dustin, you know I didn't become a father until I was 35, so you have plenty of time to ruin your life, my friend," Troy said with a smile on his face.

Christina whipped around and looked at him. "Hey, what do you mean ruin your life?"

"I was joking, sweetheart, I love being a dad." He then silently mouthed the word "kinda" at Dustin, while he blocked his face so Christina couldn't see.

She pointed at Troy's hand. "Wait, what was that?"

Troy waved his hand. "Oh, nothing, honey. What do you say we grab ourselves some drinks? I could use one after today."

Dustin smiled. "Yeah, a drink sounds great. Speaking of which, how'd your day go, Christina?"

"It was nothing outside of the ordinary. Work went well and then coming home to our bundle of joy is always a fun energy drainer."

Troy looked at Christina. "Tell me about it. I had to deal with the little guy all day. What I would give to be the one working and not being the stay-at-home dad."

She glared at him. "Troy, honey, not in front of company. We talked about this."

Dustin put his arm around Christina. "So how about that drink?"

Christina clapped her hands. "Yes, of course!"

Christina walked outside to the garage to grab three beers from the refrigerator. She came back in and handed Troy and Dustin a drink. They all sat around the kitchen bar with ENN on. Christina pointed at the TV, "Wait, is ENN is talking about The Times?"

Dustin squinted his eyes. "It looks like it."

She looked at Troy, who had the remote. "Sweetheart, could you turn up the volume?"

The host was talking about The Times' video, and then they played it from start to finish. After it was done, Christina turned around and stared at Dustin.

Dustin smiled. "Wow, that actually came across a lot better than I thought it would. Reach sure knows what they're doing."

Christina put her hand on her hip. "Who is Reach?"

"A company we are working with at The Times."

"Doing what?"

"I can't talk about it. I could lose my job if I did."

"What? I'm your sister, Dustin. Tell me now."

Dustin paused for a second. "Look, I just can't tell you, okay?"

As Christina was about to respond, the doorbell rang and it was the pizza deliveryman.

Troy looked back at the front door. "Christina, do you mind getting that so I can catch up with my main man, Dustin?"

"Sure, no problem, I'll be right back." She walked over to the front door to pay for the pizza.

While she was away, Dustin leaned over to Troy. "Thanks for that, man."

He patted Dustin on the back. "No problem. I could see what type of storm was coming in. It's always best to deflect as much as you can in a situation like that."

"Helps prevent the hurricane arguments, am I right?"

"Right you are, sir."

Christina came back with the pizza and set it down on the kitchen counter. She grabbed some plates, silverware and the salad she made, and placed it all on the counter. "Okay, guys, dig in." They each took their turns grabbing a few pieces of pizza and dishing up salad.

Christina was the first to dish up her plate and brought some wine into the dining room. She took a bite of pizza. "Don't think we're done talking about this ENN stuff, Dustin."

He glanced at Troy, who gave him a reassuring look. The two of them walked into the dining room and sat down. Troy took a bite of pizza. "How has work been going, Dustin?"

With his mouth full, Dustin replied, "Work has been going well lately. It feels like we've been in the middle of some big changes, but overall, things are really just the same as before."

Troy drank some wine. "Like what kind of changes?"

"Oh, you know, just some process, review, and execution things, nothing earth shattering."

Christina adjusted her glass. "Wait, why did you say big

time, but I guess I've just gotten used to them. It's no big deal. I don't know why I said big changes." changes, then?"

"They just seemed big at the

Troy looked over at Max. "Well, I kind of know what you mean. Our little one spoke his first word the other day and it felt like the Earth moved a little bit. In reality though, it was just one word."

"He said his first word? What was it? It was Dustin, wasn't it?"

Troy laughed and said to Dustin. "No, it was boo."

Dustin nodded. "Ah yes, of course."

The three of them laughed and continued to eat. As they were finishing dinner, Max woke, crying.

"I'll grab him." Christina got up from her seat and walked over to Max's crib. Once Max settled down, she brought him over to the table.

"Hey, little man." Dustin said as Max stared back with a wondrous smile.

Troy looked at Max. "He seems to like you, Dustin."

"He's adorable, guys. Unfortunately, though, looks like he takes after his father in the looks department."

Troy looked at Dustin with a smirk. "Yeah, let's hope he's got a better sense of humor than his uncle."

Christina checked her phone. "So Dustin, you remember my friend Jennifer, right?"

"Yeah, what about her?"

"She caught her 16 year-old son up at 5 a.m. smoking weed outside of her house with his friends. Can you believe that?"

"That is amazing. I can't believe her son woke up at 5 a.m. I wouldn't have been up that early when I was his age." Dustin said as he finished his slice.

She rolled her eyes. "That's not what I meant, Dustin. You're missing the point here."

"Oh, come on, it's not like he's the first kid in the history of the Earth to smoke pot. I wouldn't be surprised if he had been doing it long before then. I mean, when there's smoke there's pot."

"Bad choice of words, man," Troy said laughing.

She put her phone down. "That's not funny, Troy. Stop laughing."

Troy looked at Christina. "Lighten up a bit, it is kind of funny. Heck, I smoked weed when I was 15."

"You what?"

Dustin took a bite of salad. "Easy, Christina, we're all adults here and it's not like we all haven't done a little something we shouldn't have at one point or another in our lives. No need to roast your husband or put him on trial just because he's trying to relate to a teenager. There's nothing wrong with that, and in fact, it's something you're eventually going to have to do with Max."

"True."

Whispering across the table to Troy, Dustin said, "Don't worry man, I dig it. It's funny."

Still holding Max, she wiped the drool from his mouth. "We've kicked the can far enough down the street, it's time to tell us what this whole ENN thing is about."

Dustin took a bite of pizza. "What do you mean, Christina?"

"First, this report about Revision came out just this morning and then by the time the evening comes around, you guys have several interviews with Horizon executives cleverly bashing Revision, while promoting Horizon? How could you have possibly gotten access to them so quickly? How could they have gotten into Newbury, when they are located in Paris? Don't get me wrong, Dustin. I'm not condoning what Revision did in any way, but it's just weird and suspicious how quickly The Times could create such a story."

Dustin scooted his chair back from the table. "I understand that might seem fishy to you, but the executives were in town, the two sides connected, they arrived to our office quickly, and we were able to make a great video. I'd say that's impressive, wouldn't you, Troy?"

"I guess so."

She adjusted Max's shirt. "Hey don't take his side, you know what I'm saying is justified."

Troy nodded. "Well, yeah, but don't you think you're jumping to conclusions a little too quickly?"

"I'll admit, I'm maybe a bit impulsive, but you have to jump in the ring with me on this one, Dustin. I can smell what's going on here, and it's not good."

Dustin looked behind him. "I went to the bathroom before I got here and I swear I wore a diaper."

Troy laughed.

"Why can't you take what I'm saying seriously?" Christina asked.

"Okay, I'm sorry. But could you be a little more specific or direct with what you're trying to get at? So what, we had Horizon executives in our office at an opportune time to create a video talking about the Revision news, as well as how Horizon may or may not be different. What's wrong with that?"

Max was finally asleep in her arms, so Christina whispered, "Oh please, don't act like you weren't paid to spew that crap."

"Even if we were, do you think I'd be able to talk about it?" Dustin said.

Christina gave her husband a look motioning to the upstairs. "Troy, can you take Max and put him to bed?"

"Sure, sweetheart, let me take him from you."

He picked up Max and walked upstairs.

Prior to returning, Troy walked into the kitchen to grab a new bottle of wine and then sat back down to join Christina and Dustin once more. "More wine, anyone?" He said as he yanked the cork out of the bottle.

Christina looked up at him. "I'm pretty sure the last thing we need around this fire is more gasoline."

"It's wine, not gas, honey."

Dustin held his wine glass. "I know what you're saying, Christina. Don't worry, we can be civilized. I'd love some more wine, Troy. Thanks for asking."

Troy poured Dustin a new glass, followed by his own. He looked at Christina and she stared back at him. "There ya go, babe. A little wine goes a long way for the soul."

Christina sighed with a smile. "Thank you, Troy."

"So are we off the whole work controversy thing and can we talk about something else?" Troy said.

"No, Troy. We're not finished talking about this."

Dustin took a sip of his wine. "What else is there to say?"

Christina rested a hand on the table. "Okay, let's just say, hypothetically, The Times is getting paid by Horizon to broadcast their marketing BS. What happened to you? I thought you were a journalist."

"First of all, we're not getting paid by them and even if that was remotely true, which it's not, it wouldn't be that obvious."

She shook her head. "I thought you were better than this, Dustin. I thought you had ethics. I thought you knew how to do the right thing."

"Since when do you care about ethics and doing things the right way? You work for an insurance company, for goodness sakes."

Christina slapped her hand on the table. "Do not disrespect what I do for a living. People know exactly what I do, there's no deception at my job. We tell people everything they are going to get, when they work with us."

Dustin drank more of his wine. "Debatable."

Troy leaned back in his chair. "Yeah, I'm going to have to agree with Christina on this one."

"We are not getting paid to promote Horizon."

"Dustin, it's okay if you are. We're your family and won't say anything to anyone. We're not going to blame you for doing your job. Just don't lie to us, is all we're asking. This type of thing is out of your control anyway, and we would never hold it against you," he said.

"Thanks, Troy."

Christina took a deep breath. "Look, just be honest with us, and I'll let this go."

"If I am, you two have to promise on your son's life that you tell no one about this. If anyone finds out that I leaked this information, my career will be over."

"You can trust us, right, Christina?" Troy said as he looked over at her.

"Yes, you can trust us, Dustin."

He paused for a moment. "Okay, yes, we are under contract with Horizon."

Christina folded her arms. "I knew it."

Troy held out his hand. "Okay, it's out there now. Thank you for telling us and thank you for being honest with us, Dustin."

"Yeah, it's out there," Dustin said as he looked around the room.

Troy leaned forward in his seat. "Look, Dustin, I know we haven't gotten to know each other like we had planned to, but let me give you some advice. Get away from The Times. Get away as fast as you can. It's a foregone conclusion that people are going to find out about this. My wife saw through that video easily, and this was the first time she had seen it. She's not in journalism, for crying out loud. People are going to find out about this soon, and when they do, The Times will end. You don't want to be around when that place comes crumbling down. I know it seems hard, but you have to make a change, Dustin."

Dustin threw his arms up. "And go where? The industry is shrinking and so are its jobs. The Times is an anomaly in the market and while I've done good work in my career, I'm not a Pulitzer winner. I'm above average and that doesn't equal job offers in a shrinking market. If I lose this job, I will have nowhere to go, so this is what I have to do in order to make my living."

Troy shook his head. "That's not true. You have plenty of places to go. You are a very talented person, Dustin. I think you'd be great in marketing because you have such a creative mind, but waiting around for this bomb to go off may blackball you, not only from journalism, but from other industries as well."

"I just can't leave. I don't know where to go or what to do. It isn't that easy for someone like me, Troy. Journalism is all I know, and I can't abandon it now."

Troy finished his wine and paused for a moment. "By staying with this, Dustin, you might as well be abandoning it."

Chapter 10

People were enthralled with the coverage and many ended up signing new contracts with Horizon as a result. During the evening two days later, David called up Jack while he was at home.

"Hey, Jack, how's it going this evening? It's David from Horizon."

Jack muted the TV before he spoke. "Pretty good, just sitting at home watching a movie. How's your evening going?"

"Good. Listen, I just wanted to say thanks for getting that first video up the other day, it's great that we were able to get this program off the ground so quickly."

Jack took a sip of water. "I agree. It wasn't perfect, but we'll be better with our next video. Did you have any suggestions for what we could do better with our next one?"

"I did, actually. I want to see these features blur the lines between promotion and independent news even more. What your team did with the first video was nice, but I want them to really convince the audience that they are still journalists. I want them to challenge what our employees are saying. I want them to be more prepared for each interview. This first video was too soft and I think some viewers detected that."

Jack changed the channel on his TV. "No problem at all, David. We can absolutely get that done in our next feature. We already have half of the history clips done, and should have the rest finished within a few days."

"I heard from Reach that those were in, happy to see your team is being productive."

Jack shifted in his seat. "So, did you have any ideas for what our next reactive video would be?"

"I know exactly what I want. My wife is involved with a local charity in Paris and her organization has been receiving some flak due to remarks from American celebrity actress Monique Robinson. What she is saying is basically false, and her non-profit is in the running for a bid my wife's company needs. I need you to put her in her place."

Jack scratched his head. "What does that have to do with the contract we signed?"

"With the amount of money we are paying The Times, you should listen to me. I don't think Eric would appreciate losing our support just because you couldn't work with us. We need you all to produce reactive content about Monique Robinson, so it's time to react."

Jack sat forward. "Relax, David. There's no need to make threats or inferences like that." He took a breath. "So what do you want us to say about her?"

"I want you to shut her up. Everyone has skeletons in their closets, so find Monique's."

Jack's eyes wandered. "Where do we even start on something like that?"

"You're a journalist, aren't you?"

Jack rolled his eyes, but didn't respond.

"Exactly. You'll figure it out. And if you don't, use your imagination. After all, The Times is the news, isn't it?"

"Yeah. We'll get it done. Don't worry about a thing."

Jack got into work the next day and began searching for information about Monique. He came upon a story where she punched a reporter who was trying to interview her at a movie premiere. Jack found another story regarding an arrest she had for driving under the influence of alcohol, though she never had any charges formally filed against her. Finally, he read about the divorce she went through three years back.

"Oh, yes, we have our feature now," Jack muttered to himself.

Jill, Dustin, and Cameron all arrived at 7 a.m. and went to their workspaces. An hour later, Jack walked over to them. "Be in the conference room in 5 minutes, we have our next piece of reactive content."

All three of them gathered up their things and met Jack in the conference room.

Jack passed out his notes to the three of them. "Sit down, be quiet, and listen to what I have to say. I had an unpleasant conversation with David Reid last night, and I have to say he was not overly excited about our first video."

Jill had a puzzled look on her face. "What do you mean, he wasn't excited?"

Jack lowered his head. "He was not happy with the performances from you three. David thought you all were unconvincing as journalists and he wants to see more doubt in the next set of interviews."

Dustin let out a subtle laugh and smirked. "Well, we are not really journalists, and we are crossing a fine line here. In this situation, you can't have your cake and eat it too."

Jack thought for a second. "Don't let this go to your head, Dustin, but I think you're right."

Cameron searched through the notes. "Why again do we have to have those executives in the features to begin with? They just complicate things. Let's just cut out the middlemen, because we don't need those suits to get this job done."

Jack had a surprised look on his face. "You really think not having Horizon executives in these videos is going to help?"

Cameron nodded. "I think it's the best adjustment any of us can make at this point. Let us stand by ourselves when we're in front of that camera. It will be more definitive that way."

Jack tapped his chin. "I like that idea. I'll go ahead and let Horizon know of our change and then we can get started on today's video."

Jack sent a quick email to his contacts at Horizon, including David Reid. He received a response five minutes later confirming that Cameron's new idea was accepted.

Jill looked at her notes. "Oh, yeah, Jack, you said you wanted to get in on this video, right? Why don't you take my place?"

Jack hesitated. "No, that's okay. From the conversation I had with David last night, I think it's best that you three remain in this video, not me. After all, we're trying to simplify things, right?"

"Suit yourself," Jill said as she shrugged her shoulders.

"So in what direction are we taking the reactive content today?" Dustin asked.

"Monique Robinson."

Jill threw her hands up. "What?"

Cameron cleared his throat. "Can you elaborate further on that?"

Jack searched through his notes. "I absolutely can. Our job today is to make sure we hang this woman's dirty laundry high and dry for the entire world to see."

Cameron tapped the table with his finger. "And what does that have to do with our Horizon deal?"

Jack looked back at him. "Absolutely nothing, except that it has everything to do with it. This is a head of the company assignment, and we need to be successful with it. Now that you know this has to do with Horizon, I am going to assign each of you a part of this feature to create. Make sure you add some entertainment value to these."

"Entertainment value?" Jill asked.

Jack sat forward in his seat. "Yes. Generate intrigue, invoke emotion from viewers, make them cry, make them laugh, shock them. That's the kind of entertainment value I'm talking about. I want this feature to burn a permanent hole in people's minds."

"Okay, Jack," Jill said.

Jack pointed at each of them. "Cameron, your job is to find out every single detail about Monique's divorce, which happened three years ago. Dustin, she punched out a reporter at one of her movie premieres. Get some quotes from that reporter and make that situation seem like it was yesterday. Jill, she was arrested for driving under the influence of alcohol a while back, but no charges were brought against her. Make that hurt. Make all of it hurt."

The three of them stood up and walked back to their desks to get to work.

Jack sat back down in the conference room and stared out the window as clouds rolled in blocking the sunshine. A moment later he got up from his seat and returned to his office.

The two family lawyers who worked on Monique's divorce had a bad falling out. This allowed Cameron to obtain records and the case file from one of the disgruntled lawyers, anonymously.

Jill called the Newbury Police Department and collected a copy of the police report that was filed the night Monique was arrested. Jill discovered that the police confiscated over $4,000 from Monique that night. The report claimed she was driving to obtain drugs before they pulled her over. Civil Forfeiture was the rule under which the officers could confiscate the cash, but Jill still found it odd that they would drop the DUI charge, especially when her blood alcohol level was .12 over the legal limit.

Dustin found the name of the man who was hit by Monique. The reporter was soon fired after the situation with Monique. He told Dustin the reason why she punched him. After she said no more questions, he asked, "My daughter wants to be an actress. Do you have tips for any young aspiring actresses out there?" After he asked the question, Monique turned around and knocked him out with one punch. Dustin gathered a few other quotes from him.

Two hours had passed and Jack walked over to his three editors. "Are you all ready to start shooting? The film crew is almost here."

They got up from their desks and waited for Horizon's team to arrive. 10 minutes later the film crew arrived in the office and set up a different set this time. They put up a painted background of Newbury's skyline, where the green screen would have gone, and in front of it they placed a desk with The Times logo on the front.

Cameron pointed at the set. "What in the world is this, Jack?"

"This is the new direction we're headed in, since we decided to cut Horizon's executives from the video. Are you ready to go first, Jill?"

"Yeah, I'm ready to go."

Jack nodded at the stylist. "Make sure you get some makeup done before you get up there, and then we can begin."

After getting her makeup done, Jill came back and said, "Okay, Jack. I'm ready. Can we get started?"

"Get up there." Jack put up his hand. "And we're rolling in three, two, one, action!"

"Hello, my name is Jill Reddick and this is The Times. Our top story tonight is Monique Robinson and the past you don't know. My co-anchors will be on shortly, but to start, we're going to take you through a run-in Monique had with authorities six months ago. She was pulled over by a Newbury Police Department highway patrolman and did not pass the field sobriety test that was given on site. Monique was then arrested, with her blood alcohol level being .12 over the legal limit, though she was ultimately not charged with a DUI."

Jill continued speaking as she looked at a monitor playing a video in front of her.

"As if the fact that she was not charged with a DUI wasn't suspicious enough, The Times acquired a copy of the police report. The report showed the arresting officer confiscated $4,000 in cash from Robinson and claimed it under Civil Forfeiture."

A second video played while Jill kept speaking. "The Times contacted the Newbury Police Department for comment on the cash seizure, but they declined."

"While it's conceivable the cash confiscated from Robinson was just part of the officer doing his job, an anonymous source told The Times that Robinson used the cash to pay off the officer in order to avoid a DUI charge. It's uncertain where the truth lies in this matter, but you can be sure we will follow up on any leads we have. We'll be right back." The camera stopped and Jill left the set.

Jack smiled as he walked over to shake Jill's hand. "Great job, way to start us off on the right foot. Cameron, you are next. Ready?"

"Yep," he said as he walked onto the set.

"Welcome back, my name is Cameron Nelson and this is The Times. In the second part of our story, we took a closer look at the divorce between Monique and her husband, Dante, that happened three years ago."

A video summarizing the divorce aired as Cameron watched it. It was reported that Dante had cheated on Monique and had been stockpiling money in an overseas bank account where she could not access it. Coverage from various news outlets painted Monique as the victim.

Cameron folded his hands together. "As you all know, Dante ended up not getting any of the money from the marriage due to his alleged affair. Earlier today, The Times learned of a sworn affidavit that never made it into the legal proceedings. Shay Morrison, who worked on a daytime soap opera with Robinson for the four years prior to this event, disclosed that he and Monique had an affair of their own during Monique and Dante's marriage."

Another video slowly went through the affidavit on screen, but Cameron continued talking this time. "We reached out to Monique's representatives to see if they had any comment on the matter, but they declined to say anything at this time."

"While the divorce between the former couple was undoubtedly a difficult time for them, Monique may have been just as responsible for the breakup as her ex-husband Dante was."

"Now it's time for us to take a break, and we will be back with Dustin Smith, who will tell you about a time when Monique's impatience cost a man his job. Stay tuned."

The camera stopped rolling and Jack raised his hands. "Yes! That's what I'm talking about, Cameron! Boy, your stock is rising like mercury on a hot day."

"Easy, Jack. You're infringing upon my territory. Stick to what you know, and what you know is being Jack Strain," Dustin said.

Jack laughed. "No, you're right. But what do you expect? I spend all of this time around you; some of your BS is bound to seep into me."

Dustin looked away. "Got that visual, Jill?"

She shook her head. "Yeah, I'll be throwing up in the bathroom. Get going, Dustin."

Dustin slapped Jack on the back. "Well, I'm ready! You ready to do this, Strain pain?"

"Be quiet and sit down, please," Jack said as he pointed to the set. "Okay, loudmouth, time to walk your talk. Three, two, one, action!"

"And we're back here at The Times. My name is Dustin Smith. The last part of our Monique Robinson profile takes a look at the punch heard round Hollywood."

An old news report explaining the situation aired, while commentary from Dustin continued in the background.

"While you can look at this situation and say, 'Of course Monique punched that guy out, she gets hounded every day and he had to have been harassing her. Good for her to stand up to abuse like that'. Well, not so fast, Captain Jumps to Conclusions. There is more to this story than meets the eye, and no that's not a pun."

"A few hours ago, we reached out to the reporter who was struck by Monique that night. He told The Times his side of the story. Apparently, Robinson had answered enough questions and said, 'That's all the questions for tonight.' Reporter Martin Paige then asked if she had tips for any young aspiring actresses out there when Robinson whipped around and struck Martin in the head."

Dustin paused, while a video aired, showing still shots of the theater where the event took place.

"Three days after Martin was hit by Monique, he was unceremoniously fired from his job. Paige believes his reputation suffered greatly when the story broke. The Times reached out to Monique Robinson's representatives again but she declined to comment once more. It can be funny how you think a celebrity is a role model and just when you begin to dig, you learn they actually aren't. Thank you for watching The Times, I'm Dustin Smith," Dustin said. The camera stopped taping and Dustin stood up to leave the set.

Jack clapped his hands. "Bang! Absolutely masterful job, Dustin."

Dustin walked past him and patted him on the back. "I do what I do, Jacky."

Jack rubbed his chin. "What I want now is the three of you to get up there and provide a short statement summing up each of your segments. After that is done, I want Jill to give us a bottom line finish to this. Got it?"

Dustin nodded. "Got it. Cameron, I'll go first and you can follow me. Jill, you bring us home."

"Understood," Cameron said.

"Let's do it," Jill replied.

The three of them walked up on set once again and Jack stood behind the camera. "Three, two, one, action!"

Dustin put his hands in his pockets. "Welcome back. Thank you for watching this three part series on one of this country's most popular celebrities. Punch lines can be effective, while other times they can hurt someone. I think Monique would be the first one to tell you that."

Cameron looked at the camera. "So who is Monique Robinson? At this point, it's too difficult to say, but we do know that she is someone who doesn't mind having a good time, so long as monogamy doesn't get in the way."

Jill stepped forward. "We've all had one too many drinks before. It happens. The difference is those who choose to get behind the wheel, and those who do not. We've taken a trip down a road of lies and unknown realities, but always remember to question those you look up to because if you don't, you may find yourself looking down. Thank you for watching The Times this evening, we wish you a great night."

The camera stopped rolling and Jack walked up to the set clapping his hands. "My goodness, that was captivating. All three of you, phenomenal job today! In fact, I'm treating for drinks after work tonight, who would like to join me?"

"I'm in," Dustin answered.

"Let's do it," Cameron replied.

Jill shook her head. "I actually will have to pass, since I have a date tonight. Thanks for the offer, though. Have fun tonight, guys."

Jack put his arms around Dustin and Cameron. "We have our trio, fellas, meet me in the lobby once we finish up."

The video was sent in to Reach Media for editing. Jack was sent the video later that afternoon and approved it.

Once the day was over, Jill left the office and walked to the bar to meet her date. When she arrived, her date Morgan, who was a tall brunette with long hair, was already seated at the bar with a drink in hand. Jill walked over and took the seat next to her.

"Morgan, how are you doing?"

"Jill! I'm doing great. How are you? What a long day, I couldn't wait for you to get here, so that is why I'm already drinking. I hope you don't mind."

"Oh don't worry, I'd already have had two drinks if I were you." She looked at the bartender, Mike. "With that in mind, I'll do a shot of your house vodka and a beer."

Morgan looked at Jill. "So how was the day? Wait, before you answer, I just want to say that dinner last night was incredible."

"Oh my God, I know, I'm so glad we were able to finally make that happen. It was probably one of the best nights I've had in a while."

Morgan leaned forward to hear more. "So. Tell me about your day."

"It went well. We did something very different today and I think it went well. I guess it will only be a matter of time before I know."

"What happened?"

Jill took a sip of her drink and paused for a moment. "We have this client who asked us to make a video regarding an individual I never thought I'd report on. The stuff we filmed was fun and interesting, but I'm just unsure of how people will feel about it."

"Don't worry, I'm sure it'll turn out great!"

While the two continued talking, one of the TVs was on ENN and the video The Times released a few hours earlier got picked up. It played in full and the bartender decided to turn up the sound when it started.

"Shhh! Shhh! Everyone quiet! I want to hear this." The bartender yelled.

The seven-minute video played and everyone in the bar watched. After it concluded, Jill looked around to see what people thought.

Morgan leaned over to her and whispered, "What's wrong?"

"Nothing, nothing, everyone is just really quiet. I hope no one recognizes me from the video."

Morgan took a sip of her drink. "Why? That video was incredible. Your company did the right thing in finding out those details about Monique Robinson. What you did was a public service."

"Yeah, but a lot of the content in the video was unconfirmed."

Morgan brushed back her hair. "Oh, that doesn't matter. I'm sure everything will turn out to be true. Some celebrities think they are invisible, and they can get away with anything. This is a good reminder to all those people that honest companies like The Times are still looking out for the public's best interest."

With a smile on her face, Jill finished her drink and ordered another from the bartender. "I'll have another beer, Mike."

Mike turned his head to the side. "Coming right up. Wait a second, aren't you that girl from the Monique Robinson video?"

She shook her head with a smile. "No, I think you're confusing me with someone else."

Morgan laughed. "Don't listen to her, Mike, she's just being modest. She is the woman who was in that video."

"Wow! I can't believe a real journalist is sitting in my bar. I thought that industry had gone to hell, but The Times is keeping it alive. Another beer is coming right up, and don't worry, this round is on the house."

Jill looked at him. "Why, thank you, sir."

Morgan smiled. "Thanks, Mike."

"It feels great to have some recognition for the hard work I've done."

"The recognition is well-deserved," Morgan said as she leaned over to Jill to give her a kiss.

Mike placed Jill's drinks in front of her. "Everyone be quiet! We have a star on our hands. Remember Jill Reddick from the video we just watched?"

The people in the bar muttered to themselves.

"Well, she is sitting right here," Mike said as he pointed to Jill.

The bar exploded with conversation, and then people began to walk over to say hello. Some of the people shook her hand, while others thanked her for the diligent work. A few people even asked for her autograph, and she could not resist.

Mike raised a shot in the air. "See, miss, a star." He looked back at the crowd. "To Jill Reddick!"

Everyone in the bar raised their drinks and then went back to their seats.

Jill smiled at Morgan. "So enough about me and my day, how did the showing go this afternoon?"

"Oh yeah! The showing went great and actually, I have some exciting news."

Jill's voice was filled with excitement. "Well, what happened? Did they buy it?"

"Yep, they did."

"Oh my gosh, that's amazing. I'm so proud of you."

"Thanks, Jill. I feel fantastic about it. I never thought I would sell my first home after only being on the job for a month. This was a big sale and a major commission."

"I know it's outstanding! I'm so happy for you," Jill said as she leaned over to Morgan and gave her a kiss.

"Yeah, now comes the boring part of getting all of the paperwork done. What a day it's been for both of us."

Mike walked back over to Jill. "Excuse me, miss, I'm sorry to bother you again, but I just wanted to say thank you for the work you did because that's the last time I'll see any of Monique's films. You saved me from supporting a shady woman, so thank you again."

"You're very welcome, Mike."

Morgan put her arm around Jill. "Mike, doesn't she have a big action movie coming up this weekend?"

"Yeah, she does. My family and I had plans to go see it this coming Saturday, but those plans have been cancelled. No way am I going to pay to see that woman again."

"As you shouldn't. You can't trust deceptive people like her," Jill said as she sipped her beer.

Mike put his hands on the bar. "You know, Normal people like us have no way of telling what these big time celebrities are up to, and it's reliable companies like The Times we can count on to tell us the truth."

Jill nodded. "You got that right."

Morgan stood up. "Well, thanks so much for the drinks tonight, Mike. It was great to see you again."

"Always a pleasure to see you too, Morgan, and I think you may have a keeper on your hands. Don't let her get away."

"Don't worry, I won't," Morgan said as she smiled at Jill. "You ready to go get some dinner?"

Jill put her jacket on. "Yeah, let's do it."

They stepped outside and Jill said, "Wait a second, so you trust what The Times reports 100 percent of the time, right?"

"Of course."

"Really? You don't have any skepticism?"

Morgan looked back into the bar. "Why should I? You guys are journalists. Besides, you'd never lie to me." She gave Jill a kiss.

Jill thought for a second and then her eyes wandered away from Morgan. "Yeah, I guess I wouldn't."

Meanwhile, Jack was back in his apartment when he received a phone call from David Reid. "Hello?"

"Jack, you beautiful man, you!" David exclaimed.

Jack's eyes searched the floor. "Is everything okay?"

"Are you kidding? Is everything okay? Things are amazing, thanks to you."

"So you saw the video, did you?"

"You bet I did, and it is incredible. Your team hit her hard and it all worked out perfectly. I think I may have underestimated you, Jack. I am sorry if I ever doubted you, my friend."

Jack tilted his head back. "Oh, don't worry, you were just doing what would be natural for anyone in your position."

"You're right. The video has done wonders for my wife's charity and couldn't have worked out better. I couldn't take the chance that Monique's company would get the grant over my wife's charity. After they saw the video, they turned down the Robinson request immediately and awarded the grant to my wife's firm. Thanks again."

Jack scratched his head. "That's great, but you understand matters like that shouldn't usually involve The Times, right?"

"I know, but in our contract we have the final say on the type of content that is placed in these videos. While I do not expect a personal matter like this coming up again, it's important for you to remain flexible in your position."

"I can, but I would prefer that we didn't have something like this come up again."

"We'll see what we can do."

Jack shifted in his seat. "By the way, how did the Revision video turn out?"

"It actually did a lot better than I initially led you to believe. It wasn't a bad video at all, in fact, it was a great one. I just wanted to make sure you were motivated to create the next one."

"David, you never have to worry about motivation being an issue with me."

"But to answer your question more directly, yes, the video had a profound effect. We believe, because of it, we were able to gain over 100,000 new subscribers, and we have retained just about all of them since then."

Jack smiled. "Good, I'm glad we're having such a positive impact on Horizon's business."

"We are happy as well. Keep it up, Jack."

"We will. Anything else you wanted to discuss with me, David?"

"Yes." David started to speak, but then paused for a moment. "You're going to be hearing about a murder involving one of the players on the Newbury Stampede soon. It's already happened, and he's in police custody, but the story hasn't gotten out to the public yet. Be ready to create some reactive content that supports him. The native advertising disclaimer won't be attached to the video and it's not officially part of our deal, but compensation will be provided separately."

Jack thought for a second. "Understood, but can you tell me why we're doing this?"

"Horizon has a massive amount invested in the overall success of the Stampede, not to mention having bought the rights to the name of the arena, Horizon Center. Its value cannot drop in any way. This is about the bigger picture and supporting Dennis Lodge is part of that."

Jack turned his head. "So what happens if this is true and he did it? Where does that leave us?"

"You're the press, people will forgive you. They've proven that thus far."

"Yeah, I agree. People love us so much that they're unable to stop watching, no matter what we do."

David let a brief, but menacing laugh out. "That's the beauty of being the news, Jack. That's the beauty of being the absolute best and having the biggest audience. You determine, dictate, and deliver the message. I know you'll do a good job."

Jack laughed. "Oh yes, doing good work is part of the job description."

"My man, I knew I could count on you."

Chapter 11

"Today, reports are coming out of Newbury that Stampede star forward Dennis Lodge has allegedly murdered his wife and eight month old daughter. Lodge, who has had a history with alcohol abuse, made a phone call to 911 late last night. The recording has Lodge screaming at his wife and daughter, 'Why did you make me do this? Why?' His wife and daughter were both pronounced dead an hour prior to the airing of this broadcast. Lodge was arrested, eventually posting bail, which was set at $1 million. We will keep you updated with any new information as we receive it. I'm Jamie Carol, ENN."

The country exploded at the news of this apparent murder. While the jury was still out on whether or not Lodge murdered his family, the vast majority of the public had already decided he was guilty.

Jack emailed Jill, Dustin, and Cameron that day to warn them of the content they'd be producing. It was only minutes after Jack's email was sent to his team that he received a response from all three of them.

143

Dustin's email had his typical humor mixed in. "Are you freaking kidding me? I'd rather produce flattering content about Ebola than this guy."

Jill sent a reply that was cautious. "Jack, I understand this is our job and there are certain things that are out of our control, but this is something that could lead to our demise."

Cameron replied, "We've publicly smeared an actress, hell, why not defend a murderer?"

Jack sent a reply to all three. "A job is a job and a check is a check. Get your heads right and be here on time."

That day, everyone got into the office one hour before the usual start time. They all met in the conference room and Jack looked up at each of them. "First things first. The video we are going to make won't have the 'Sponsored by Horizon' disclaimer at the end. While this has been fed from them, it's not technically part of our deal. We didn't want to set off any red flags with the disclaimer in today's feature."

No one responded.

Jack shuffled some papers around. "Well, today is going to be fun."

"Fuck you, Jack," Dustin said.

Jack face filled with anger. "What?"

"I didn't stutter."

Jack's eyes widened. "Do you want to be fired?"

"Do it, meat. You won't fire me."

Jack sat back in his chair and took a deep breath. "Look, Dustin. I know you must have some misguided sense of right and wrong here, but we're just doing our job."

Dustin looked away from him. "Keep telling yourself that, meat."

As Jack was about to respond, Cameron rubbed his eyes. "It's 6:15 in the morning. You two can't bicker this early. Now look, we have to do this. Dustin, you've been fine with what we've been doing all along, so what's the problem?"

Dustin crossed his arms. "I'm fine now. Let's just get this over with."

Jack extended his hand across the table to Dustin. "Truce?"

"Truce, meat." Dustin shook his hand.

Jill looked at some notes in front of her. "So when can we get started on this?"

Jack cleared his throat. "In a moment, princess, in a moment."

Dustin looked straight at Jack. "Man, when you woke up this morning, did you say to yourself, yep, I'm going to be a jackass?"

Jack tossed his arms in the air. "I thought we had a truce."

Cutting off Dustin before he could respond, Cameron slapped the table. "Guys! Can't we all just get along?"

Jill laughed. "Gee golly gosh, Cameron. We sure can."

Jack nodded. "Okay, let's get this going so it can be done with."

They all returned to their desks, but Dustin glared at Jack as they walked back.

A few hours later, the camera crew arrived and Jack summoned his team to the common area to film. "Okay, everyone, this is where we show our true colors and demonstrate our professionalism to the entire world."

Dustin took a deep breath. "Since we're doing the same format as the last video, which of us do you want to go first?"

Jack thought for a second and looked at the three of them. "Jill, you're going first. Order has never mattered in these videos, but I want you to start because I trust you'll lead us in the right direction."

Jill nodded with a straight face.

"Lead us, Jill." Dustin said as he put his hand on her shoulder. He then glanced over at Jack. "Where am I batting at, Jackie-poo-poo?"

Jack shook his head and looked at the ground. "Go last, Dustin. Just don't screw it up."

"Words your mother said that have never come true."

Jack walked back into his office where he printed off an email from David Reid. He came back and handed notes to each of them. "Horizon sent each of you a script or at least bullet points to use for your segment. Don't say things word for word, because if you do, you will sound like a walking press release. Add in your own voice and style, but do not change the overall message. Am I clear?"

Jill looked at him. "Did you have any chance to push back on this?"

Jack smiled. "Push back on what? This is what we do, Jill. I'm counting on you."

Jill sighed. "I guess I'm ready then." After a moment, Jill took her seat on the set.

Jack stood behind the camera. "Three, two, one, action!"

"Good evening and welcome to The Times, my name is Jill Reddick. Tonight's top story is Dennis Lodge and what you don't know about him. As you have probably heard by now, Dennis Lodge has been arrested and is suspected of killing his wife and eight month old daughter."

She looked down at the monitor in front of her as a clip from ENN's broadcast played. "It's important to take reports like this with a grain of salt. In our society, suspects are innocent until proven guilty and out of respect for Lodge and his family, it's important to keep that in mind." She looked to her left with a face full of disgust.

"Stop the camera!" Jack screamed. He walked up to Jill on set and whispered to her. "I understand how you feel, but we all need to keep personal feelings out of this."

"Our jobs are to tell the truth, not be a distraction from it," Jill whispered. "We're going to hell for this, Jack. No company will hire us if what we're doing gets out."

"You're worrying about the wrong details. Your job is to do what I say. I say this is what you're doing."

He pointed at Jill as he left the set. "Pull yourself together because you're about to interview Lodge's therapist, Dr. Marcum."

Jill adjusted her hair and shifted in her seat. She took a few deep breaths and then looked at the camera.

"Three, two, one, action!"

"Dennis Lodge, who has been a star forward for the Newbury Stampede, has had a history with alcohol abuse in the past. We were able to obtain a statement from his therapist, who spoke about his current level of sobriety. Dr. Marcum told us that Lodge has been clean and sober for the past 10 years, and he had been mentoring others in AA. We are now joined by Dr. Marcum herself via satellite. Dr. Marcum, thank you for taking the time to speak with us this evening."

Dr. Marcum looked at her. "Thank you for having me on."

"So with 10 consecutive years of sobriety, how likely is it that alcohol played a part in this tragic incident?"

Dr. Marcum adjusted her glasses. "For any recovering alcoholic, it can only take one time for something to happen. That said, I seriously doubt Dennis would be capable of something like this. I've known him for the past decade. During that time, his family was always the primary motivating factor for him remaining sober."

"How can you be so certain?"

"I've seen the way he's been living over the past 10 years and he continuously puts himself in situations where he wouldn't be tempted to drink. You can also take into account the fact that he has been a leader in AA for three years now. He mentors three other individuals and has been a major influence in helping them stay sober."

Jill glanced at her notes. "The last question we have this evening is what would you say to Dennis if you could speak with him right now?"

Dr. Marcum shifted in her seat. "I'd tell him to stay strong and continue in his sobriety. Dennis, you've made enormous progress during the past 10 years, and I'm confident you will successfully overcome these allegations. I'm with you 100 percent."

Jill sat back in her chair and looked at the camera in front of her. "Well, thanks once again for joining us, Dr. Marcum. We'll be right back with more on Dennis Lodge after this."

The cameras stopped recording and Jill walked off the set.

Jack raised his arms. "Yeah baby! Thata girl."

Jill walked into the kitchen without saying anything. She stayed there sipping a cup of tea and stared out the window.

Jack looked at the kitchen. "Hey Jill! You coming back?"

She didn't respond.

Jack shrugged his shoulders and looked at Cameron. "You ready, big man? You're up next."

"Oh, I'm ready." Cameron gave Jack a high-five and then walked on set to sit down. "Start it up, Jack."

Jack walked over to the cameraman. "Three, two, one, action!"

"Hello, and welcome back to The Times, I'm Cameron Nelson. Often times, the best way to get a true idea of a situation is to talk with the person who is in the middle of it. While we can't speak to Dennis Lodge himself, we are able to talk with one of his former teammates. Joining us this evening is former Haste center, Dominic Cooper. Dominic, thanks for being with us tonight."

Staring back at the camera with sunglasses on and a sandy beach behind him was Dominic Cooper. In his thick New York accent, he responded, "Not a problem, Cameron. How are you doing this evening?"

"I'm fine, thank you. So you played with Dennis Lodge for six years. Both of you were on two of Newbury's championship teams, so you probably knew things about him that other people didn't. What was he like as a teammate?"

Dominic took a sip from the cup of water he had sitting next to him. "Lodgy was the best teammate I could ask for. I didn't know much about his personal life, but we were best friends when it came to the Stampede."

"Well, let's focus on that. During your time with him, did you ever see him drink in the locker room, at a party, or anything like that?"

Dominic cracked his neck. "Look, anybody I've ever played with is part of a brotherhood, and I'm no rat, okay? But to answer your question, I never saw Lodgy drink in the locker room or at a party. He was always a super conservative guy, like he was afraid of something."

"So what would you say are the odds that he would kill his wife and eight month old daughter?"

Dominic threw his hands up in the air. "I know he loved his family very much and can't imagine the type of grief he's going through right now. The Dennis I knew would never think of killing anyone, let alone his own family. I think professional athletes like him get thrown under the bus too easily and don't always get due process. I'm no expert, but if I was a betting man, I'd bet Lodgy didn't do this, and it was something or someone else that's responsible for this great tragedy."

"All of us here at The Times share the same sentiment, and thank you again for your time."

"Of course, it's no problem. I'm happy to do it."

Cameron shuffled some papers on the desk and then looked at the camera. "That concludes part two of our story this evening. We'll be right back with more on Dennis Lodge."

Jack was bowing. "Yes, Cameron. Yes."

Cameron smiled.

Jill walked over to Cameron. "I see you had no problem with that."

He crossed his arms. "Just doing my job, and doing it well."

Jack clapped loudly one time. "This is it. The home stretch is here. Dustin, you're on third base and you need to score. You want to score. You will score."

Dustin rolled his eyes as he walked on the set. "Put a sock in it, Jack. I've got a date with a bottle of whiskey and I do not want to be late."

"I knew you'd come around. Three, two, one, action!"

"Good evening and welcome back to The Times, I'm Dustin Smith. We do not have any experts or friends to talk to in this segment, you just have me."

He moved some papers aside.

"Our justice system says that a suspect is innocent until proven guilty, but our society's perceptions indicate the opposite. It's easy to be cynical about people like Dennis Lodge and say athletes are nothing but rich morons who think they are invincible and can get away with anything, but perhaps we're looking at this the wrong way."

Dustin glanced at his notes.

"Professional athletes are big targets for plenty of things in this world. They can be victimized and major assumptions can be made. I'm not saying they are incapable of committing a crime or are above reproach when it comes to their lives, but shouldn't we treat them like we would any other member of society? We all have our assumptions of Mr. Lodge, but until we discover the true facts of the situation, live your lives without judgment, ignore it, and wait for our reliable justice system to deliver just that, justice."

The camera did a wide zoom-out on Dustin. "Thank you all very much for watching and good night."

The camera stopped and Jack approached Dustin to hug him, who ducked away from it.

Jack stood there with his arms extended. "Come on, just one."

Dustin kept walking. "Hell no."

The film crew packed up their gear and left the office.

Jack and his team returned to the conference room.

Dustin leaned forward in his seat. "So, meat, where do we go from here? What happens next? Should we expect to be defending rebel armies carrying out genocide next?"

Jack glared at Dustin. "If that's what our client wants."

The four of them waited for the final cut of the video from Reach Media and then watched it together.

Dustin shook his head in disbelief. "Damn, Reach sure knows how to make this stuff compelling. I suppose that's what happens when a plan comes together, right, Jacky?"

Jack let out a brief laugh. "This is what we've been working towards. When I wanted to change what the journalism industry was and could be, this was the summit I was hoping for. What power this has. The world will have no choice but to say yes and crave for more."

Jill adjusted her shirt. "Do you really think the world is going to buy into this stuff? It's just camouflaged chatter about a secondary, separate issue at hand. This deflects from the main story of Lodge murdering his family. I think people are smart enough to understand that. Cameron?"

"It's impressive, there's no denying that."

Dustin's head was resting on his hand. "I mean, I believe it. This is good stuff, even though we know the guy did kill his family."

Jack glared at Dustin. "Allegedly. Come on now. Don't give in to the tendency we all have to condemn a man before he is given due process."

Dustin raised one eyebrow. "Due process, Jack? The man killed his family with a fire poker. The only process he should go through is getting hooked up to the electric chair."

"Easy, Dustin," Cameron said in a relaxed tone.

Dustin moved his chair back from the table. "This whole situation just has its head up its ass."

Jack gave his approval to Reach Media, as did Horizon, and the video was distributed. They all left the office and went home for the evening.

Chapter 12

The video went viral as soon as it hit the web. Within one day, the video received over 10 million views and was being played on every network imaginable. The Times' video about Lodge was seen as defense for his behavior. The public was seriously questioning the independence of the report, and press inquiries for interviews were flooding the emails of everyone at The Times.

Jack woke up the next morning and went about his daily routine. He picked up The Metro that morning and noticed the headline. "The Times Defends Alleged Murderer In New Video."

As Jack read through the article, the author questioned The Times' motives to produce a video that largely avoided the fact that Lodge was the prime suspect for the murder of his wife and child. The article went on to criticize the manner in which the video deflected attention away from the murder and focused on other aspects of Lodge's life.

Since the video went live the night before, Jack's email was stuffed full with hundreds of requests for an interview. Among the interview requests Jack saw, one was sent by the senior editor and lead anchor at ENN, Carrie Woodson.

Jack picked up the phone and called Eric Peterson.

"Hello?" Eric answered.

"Eric, listen to me, ENN wants to interview us about the Lodge video. What should we do?"

Eric took a deep breath. "This is unexpected, without a doubt. You know what our policy is for people requesting an interview though."

"True, but since my email account has over 300 different interview requests, we may want to get in front of this."

"Let's not be impulsive about this, yes, this is the biggest and, some could argue, the most negative reaction we've seen, but that doesn't mean we need to fold and let the world in on what we're doing."

"But wasn't that our hope in the first place? To be the first ones to tell the world about our deal with Horizon?"

Eric sighed. "Yes, that's true. We ideally wanted to be the first ones to step in front of a story like that, but people don't think we're getting paid to produce content for Horizon. They're just pissed we are producing videos that support Dennis Lodge."

Jack threw a hand in the air. "Oh, so you think there's no way publications are going to make a connection between us and Horizon working together? Did you not see the ridiculous ad with Dennis and David that aired during the video? People aren't that stupid."

"You're right, they aren't that stupid, but they are that gullible."

Jack put his hand on his forehead. "Jeez. So what about the ENN interview then?"

Eric paused to think. "Look, I will speak with David about this, and then we'll let you know how we're going to proceed with all the interview requests. Just so you know, I'd be shocked if we agreed to an interview at all, but if we did, it'll be on a big stage and it'll only be a onetime thing. Does that make sense?"

"Yes. Let me know what you decide." He hung up the phone and sat back in his chair. Once Jack had finished eating breakfast, he grabbed his briefcase and drove into work.

As Jill was driving into work, she came to a red light and saw people staring at her from the car beside hers. The light turned green and as she accelerated, the people flipped her off and sped away.

"What in the world?" Jill said to herself.

While Cameron was driving to work that morning, he listened to the news as he usually did. The weather report came on for the day, followed by top news stories, but today, the only news story was about the Lodge video from the night before.

A brief audio clip of a journalist talking about the video was aired. "I have no idea what The Times is thinking. This is a story where you either go hard against Lodge or stay a million miles away from it. It was a landmine with a giant flag in front, and The Times stepped right on it. It's baffling that they published the video and makes one wonder what's really going on inside of that place," the reporter said.

Cameron began to look around to make sure no one recognized him. He slumped down into his seat as he drove into work.

"Wow, there usually are five top news stories, and now we are the only one. This is going to be a bad day," Cameron said to himself.

Dustin didn't park in the The Infinity Building's parking lot that morning and instead parked two blocks away. He wanted to enjoy walking through the quiet city early in the morning, since it helped him get in the right mindset for the day. As he walked along, people who were walking nearby noticed him and were glaring his way.

One man stared straight at Dustin as he walked past. "You suck."

Dustin blinked. "Come again?"

"You and that company you work for suck. How could you defend Lodge? How much did you get paid for that?"

Dustin pointed to himself. "First of all, I wasn't defending Lodge. If anything, I was merely pointing out the general public's tendency to convict a person before they even have a fair trial."

"Are you kidding me? Anyone with a brain knows you were defending the guy. I can't wait to see The Times close because of this. It's going to be sweet."

Dustin smiled. "I seriously doubt that'll happen. In case you haven't noticed, we're bigger than any newspaper, magazine, or website in the world. The Times is an institution and isn't going anywhere anytime soon."

The man stormed off in anger and Dustin started to walk faster toward The Infinity Building. While no one else said anything to him, other people were glaring at Dustin intensely.

Jack walked into the office to find people yelling across the room, nearly all employees were talking on the phone with journalists wanting an interview with someone at The Times. What was usually a quiet, calm office had become the center of chaos. He walked into his office and shut the door as he tried to regain his bearings.

Meanwhile, Dustin, Jill, and Cameron were busy answering phone calls from bloodthirsty journalists and writers who were all trying to get the inside track on the story.

"Hello, this is The Times," Jill answered. "No, I'm sorry we're not taking any interviews at this time, but should that change we'll be sure to reach out to you."

Jack had sent each of them statements to provide on The Times' behalf when speaking with the press.

Dustin tossed aside the piece of paper. "Hello, this is The Times." He listened to the inquiry. "Have you ever heard of a man named Sisyphus?"

The person on the line responded yes.

"Oh great, well let me know when he gets that rock to the top of the hill because then and only then can you have an interview with us."

Jill put down her phone.

"Hello, this is The Times," Dustin said. "Remember Jimmy Hoffa's dead body? Go find it, take two pictures, one of them with a stuffed animal next to it, and then email the photos to me. Then and only then can you have an interview with us."

Jill looked at him, mesmerized. "What is wrong with you? We're supposed to be sticking to the script. You're going to put us in a bad position."

Dustin smirked at Jill. "I don't know about that. Something tells me Hoffa's dead body won't turn up and Sisyphus won't get that rock up on the hill. Just saying."

Cameron put his phone down. "I swear you two are like a married couple sometimes. Hey, Jill, why don't you just stick to your phone calls and not worry about Dustin?"

Jill pointed at him. "But he's not doing what Jack asked us to do."

Cameron nodded. "True, but we're talking with second-rate bloggers and low-level journalists, so relax. Dustin, God you're weird."

Dustin pressed the mute button on his phone. "Actually, I think witty is the word you're looking for."

Cameron turned around and ignored Dustin as he started taking phone calls again.

Jack's phone rang and as he was about to ignore it, he saw it was Eric calling. He quickly picked up the phone. "Eric, tell me you have some good news."

"Well, it's nice to hear from you too. I hope you're having a nice morning."

"Cut the chit-chat, my people are getting blown up left and right in here, and I need to give them some concrete answers. What are we doing?"

"We have a plan, but remember Jack, this is the Internet. Things come up every day that make people angry and they always forget about it."

Jack tapped his desk. "Yes, that's true for most things, but this isn't just an Internet outrage deal. 24-hour news networks are covering this story. ENN is all over it and when stuff likes this gets broadcast over there, it has staying power. Things like this get shoved down the world's throat day after day after day. It's not going to go anywhere, Eric. We need to do something, and it needs to be more than just saying, wait for it to blow over."

"Relax for a second, Jack. Everything is okay. I spoke with David, and we would like you to sit down with ENN and participate in a video interview with them. Can you do that?"

Jack hesitated. "Yes, I can do that, but what do you want me to say? I can talk, but what details am I supposed to be sharing here?"

"Just use big, generic, gray phrases that do not pin us into a corner where they can then ask you something specific. Stay on the outside with your answers and keep them asking big questions. Remember, you don't have to answer anything you're not comfortable with."

"You speak of participating in an interview like it's an art form?"

"Well, in a way it is. An interview is like a tennis match, and the person who takes charge ultimately decides how it turns out. Just keep them on their toes, reacting to you, not the other way around. Drop hints and make them think they're receiving specifics, but really, you've revealed nothing at all. Keep things specifically broad, do you know what I mean?"

Jack wrote a few thoughts down on a notepad. "I kind of see what you're saying, but I could use some examples, if possible."

"Not a problem at all. I'll have our PR team create a sample Q&A for you to review. Sink your teeth into those until you have the right mindset for what we're going for. Once you feel comfortable enough to get into an interview environment, we'll connect with ENN and set up a time. Okay?"

Jack nodded. "Okay, I like your plan. I do know where we're going, but I want to make sure I don't fumble anything. Have PR send over that Q&A as soon as possible."

The two of them hung up and Jack went over to his team to inform them of what was happening. Interrupting everyone who was responding to interview requests, Jack said, "Everyone, we're done taking phone calls. Do not answer anymore and let them go to voicemail. I will be doing an on-camera interview with ENN to discuss our video. Don't worry about a thing, I will lead us from here."

Jill gasped. "Are you sure that's the best thing to do?"

"Absolutely. We need to get in front of this thing and kill it now. I think the best way to do that is to get me in front of a camera, and Eric Peterson feels the same."

Cameron twirled a pencil. "Okay, so when is this interview taking place?"

"I'm not sure but it'll happen soon. Stay tuned, because it could end up being sometime today. I know we want to do the interview sooner than later, and I'm sure ENN feels the same."

Dustin gave him a high-five. "Okay, Chief, wear our feather proud and go get 'em."

Jack stared at Dustin without saying a word.

Jill moved her glance from Dustin to Jack. "In other words, good luck. We'll be rooting for you."

Jack walked back into his office and shut the door. He received an email an hour later from The Times' PR team. While looking over the sample Q&A, Jack drank a cup of coffee. "Well, these don't cover everything, but I think they will be enough to get me through the interview."

Eric called Jack one last time. "So how are you doing? ENN said they could do the interview at 5:30 tonight. Think you'll be ready?"

Jack cleared his throat. "I'm ready now."

"That's what I like to hear. Do you have any questions?"

"No, I understand what we're doing and know the interview will go well."

Eric briefly laughed. "That's my man. Well, good luck with the interview, and we'll talk after it's over. Remember, keep them on the outside and do not let them in, Jack."

"Thanks, I'll be sure to do that."

In the meantime, Dustin ignored orders and took a phone call when he saw it was Karen calling. "Hey you, what a surprise. It's great to hear from you, how are things?"

Karen let out a lone sob. "I'm doing okay. I was in town for some business and just found out that my parents have died."

"Oh no, that's awful. I'm so sorry to hear that!"

"Thanks, Dustin. Look I don't have many friends here in Newbury. Since I moved, they're all in Paris, so would you be able to meet up with me for lunch?"

Dustin looked around the office and lowered his tone. "Sure, I'd be more than happy to see you. Want to meet at the North Deli across the street from our building in 30 minutes?"

"That sounds great, thanks, Dustin," Karen said with some cheer in her voice.

Dustin left The Infinity Building and met Karen outside of the deli across the street. Karen's emotion from her parents' death was evident, as they hugged and walked into the restaurant.

After ordering lunch, the two of them sat down at a table and Dustin asked, "How are you feeling?"

"I'm doing better than I thought I would be."

"Really?" Dustin said with a tone of surprise.

She took a sip of her water. "Yeah. Don't get me wrong, I loved my parents very much. They were two very important people in my life, but we were never really that close."

"Sure."

"I do miss them very much, but I would be lying if I said I was totally broken up. I just feel numb. They never really put in the time when I was younger, and as I grew up we drifted further apart."

Dustin didn't have anything to say, so he continued to focus on her with a concerned look.

Karen paused. "What I feel most now is loneliness. I'm the only one left in my family and don't have anything to show for it, really."

"What are you talking about? You're beautiful, were an outstanding journalist, and by all accounts are a marketing genius with Horizon. How does all of that equate to nothing?"

She put her hands on the table. "It's not that it equals nothing because you're right, all of that is worth something. But what I mean is I want to have a real impact on this world."

"What do you mean?"

She paused for a moment while the waiter dropped the food off at their table. "Thank you, everything looks delicious," Karen said to the waitress as she took a bite of her sandwich. "Well, I don't know if leaving Horizon is the best thing to do right now. It's been a very stable job and something I've enjoyed, but I feel called in a different direction. With the amount of money I inherited from my parents, I have an opportunity to do something substantial."

Dustin bit into his sandwich. "I swear, every time I come here it's heaven in a sandwich. Too bad this sandwich is not a vacation resort because I'd spend two weeks in it."

Karen laughed. "Glad to see you're still weird. Don't be afraid of who you are, Dustin. The world needs more people like that."

Dustin took a sip of water. "So after inheriting all of that money, you're a billionaire, right?"

"Shhh, Dustin, I don't want people to know that. I did inherit enough money to fall into that category, yes, but I don't want anyone to know."

Dustin smiled at her. "I'd be the perfect trophy husband, really, I would be."

They both laughed and people around them looked at them.

Karen glanced at the couple nearby. "Sorry, sorry. We didn't mean to disturb you." She looked back at him. "Hilarious, Dustin. Hilarious," Karen said with a smile on her face.

"Of course I'm just kidding, but does the newly found money have anything to do with the direction you're being called in?" Dustin said as he took another bite of his sandwich.

"I can't say it doesn't have something to do with it, but it's not the main driving factor for me. I have no idea what I'll do with the money, but know I will do something, eventually." Just before she took another bite of her sandwich, she said, "Okay, enough money talk, let's talk about you."

"Well, that book isn't too long. I'm single, I'm happy, I'm still enjoying working for The Times, minus last night's video, and am staring down a beach vacation with some friends in a few months."

Karen winked at him. "You're right, that book isn't long at all."

Dustin laughed. "I would add that the video we created last night was sheer insanity. I'd rather skydive without a parachute then participate in one of those again."

Karen shifted her look at Dustin. "About that. Everyone at Horizon loved it, even though I know that must've been hell for you guys. Just between you and me, though, this is just the start. This was a test for us to see what you guys would do. I'm afraid if you didn't like last night's work, you are really not going to like what's coming."

Dustin turned his head to the side. "What do you mean?"

"I can't say exactly, because the next topic isn't final. As a journalist, though, I would hate it, which is why I'm not a journalist anymore. I'm sure glad I was fired before this began."

"Yeah, I can imagine you would have been frustrated with The Times if you were still working here."

"One thing's for sure, how Jack's interview goes will certainly tell a lot about what's going to happen in the future, trust me on that. I'd expect David and Horizon to back away quickly if there could be any repercussions for them," Karen said as she finished her sandwich. She took another sip of water and asked the waitress for the check. "My advice would be to get away from The Times, and get away now."

Dustin looked at her with a bewildered look. "Well, it's not that simple, I can't just leave. Besides, we are still the number one site in the entire world, and we have one of the best advertising deals around. What's not to love about that?"

She peeked away and then back at him. "No, you're right. Why would you want to leave that?"

He thought for a second. "Did you set a date for the funeral?"

"It's the beginning of next week, so I'll spend the rest of this one back in Paris planning everything."

"Well, if you need anything or someone to help you out, I'm here for you," Dustin said as he smiled back at her.

She began to blush and thanked him for the offer.

They got up from their seats and paid for their meal, but Karen cut in front of Dustin to pay.

"Are you sure you got this, Karen?"

"Absolutely. You paid the last time I had a life crisis, so now it's my turn to pay." She handed her credit card to the cashier. "So when is something horrible going to happen to you so I can do the consoling for once?"

Dustin laughed. "That's hilarious. I'll be sure to ask my parents when they think they'll die and get back to you."

"Don't forget to ask Eric or Jack when you'll be fired, too."

"Oh, yeah, that's right, I forgot about that one." He smiled. "Thanks for lunch. It was great to see you."

"Of course! Thank you for talking with me. The news of my parents definitely has been tough, but you've been a sweetheart again. Let me know when you're taking that beach vacation, maybe I'll tag along."

"I'd love that," Dustin replied.

As they walked out to say goodbye to each other, Dustin gave Karen a kiss.

The time for Jack's interview was creeping closer, and even though he could recite the PR answers by heart, he continued to obsess over the Q&A sheet his PR team sent over.

ENN's locally based film crew arrived at The Times' office an hour before the interview was scheduled to take place. They began to construct the set where Jack would be sitting, and chose to move some furniture around so the city of Newbury served as the backdrop. Tech equipment was spread out left and right, covering the space ENN's team had commandeered.

The producer who was on site asked to speak with Jack before the interview was scheduled to begin. "We'll need to get some last minute makeup done before you go on. When you sit down on set, we'll set up your microphone, which will be toward the top of your shirt. That will provide us with the best audio quality. Carrie has the list of pre-approved questions, which you have in your hand. Got all of that?"

"Yes."

"Jack? We're going to do a few sound checks to make sure everything works well. Make sure you give Jack an earpiece so he can hear what Carrie is saying," the man said to his assistant.

Lighting around the room exploded onto Jack's face and the camera in front of him had a red frame around it, indicating the broadcast was live.

"Good evening, my name is Carrie Woodson, and this is ENN. As you know by now, Dennis Lodge was arrested for the alleged murder of his wife and eight month old daughter. Since then, the world's largest online outlet, The Times, released one of the most talked about videos in history. Was the video released yesterday in defense of Lodge or was it something else entirely? We hope to find that out tonight."

A split screen then came up on the TV. One half of the screen featured Carrie, with Jack being shown on the other half. "Tonight, I am pleased to be joined by the Editor-In-Chief of The Times, Mr. Jack Strain. Jack, thank you for joining us this evening."

Jack looked into the camera. "It's a pleasure to be here. Thank you for having me."

Carrie looked down at her notes. "Let's just cut to the chase. Was the video The Times published meant to be taken as a defense for Lodge?"

"Absolutely not. That was far from what we were trying to do with that piece of content. Whenever we create something, we try our best to present the full picture of a story, and we felt the individuals we interviewed helped accomplish that."

"The video did not come across that way at all. There was virtually nothing said when it came to the murder of Lodge's family, not to mention there being absolutely zero balance in your 'report.' Why not interview the victim's side of the family?"

"We simply didn't want to expose their grief. While I understand everyone would like an ideal presentation with ideal people to interview, we only had a short amount of time to create the content and didn't have enough resources to interview every single person involved in the story. Again though, we strive to create the most balanced coverage possible."

Carrie took a quick glance to her left as a producer motioned to her. She then focused back on the camera. "Why did you decide to speak with his therapist? It's not like she could speak honestly, because if she did, she would have been violating confidentiality agreements."

Jack moved a bit in his seat. "It goes back to our mission and desire for every story we publish. We want to create a balanced environment for addressing sensitive topics, and we thought having Lodge's therapist on was a great way to diversify the piece."

"Why didn't your team ask more questions about his history with alcohol? Sure it's been 10 years since he had a documented alcohol relapse, but do you really believe he hasn't had one drink since then?"

Jack folded his hands. "Look, that question is pure speculation, and I don't have an answer for it."

Carrie tried to hide her frustration. "Why did your team not focus on the evidence that was found at the scene of the crime? What the police found at the scene was a bloody fire poker with Lodge's fingerprints on it, yet you didn't even come close to mentioning that."

Jack made a slight wince after she asked the question. "We could have speculated about the what if's, much like you do on this network, but we felt time and resources were better spent elsewhere. The evidence doesn't look good for Lodge, but everything is up in the air, no matter how much people want to convict him."

"His fingerprints were on the fire poker, Jack."

"Look, it doesn't make sense to discuss to death what viewers already are hearing from other outlets. It does viewers no good to continue shoving the same information down their throats over and over. We wanted to generate new information and content surrounding the story. How people react is out of our control." Jack sat back in his seat.

Carrie looked down at her notes again. "The video your company published came out just a few hours after news outlets initially reported the murder. It's almost like The Times knew what was coming and had a head start on everyone else."

Jack smiled. "Yes, we did react better than anyone else, that's part of why we're a leader in news."

"How did you come up with a video like that so quickly?"

Jack placed his arms on the armrests. "We have a number of sources and contacts at our disposal. Being the top producer of news in the world means we have strategies in place to ensure we react faster to stories than anyone else. Being quick is not a detriment, it's a benefit."

"Your company produces something, Jack, but it isn't news." Carrie sat forward with an irritated look on her face. "Tell us about the strategies you have in place. What are those?"

Jack smiled again. "If you think I'm going to disclose our company's business tactics, you're sadly mistaken."

Carrie put down her note cards. "I think it's pretty obvious what those tactics are. It may not be as easy to tell what exactly you all are doing behind the scenes, but it's clear trustworthiness isn't a top priority."

"That's a pretty bold statement coming from you and your network, Carrie."

Carrie shook her head. "Let's talk about that commercial The Times aired with David Reid and Dennis Lodge. Interesting timing to have that air right in the middle of your video, wouldn't you agree?"

"That ad has been playing on plenty of networks aside from our own videos. It was just an advertisement, same as the ones you air on this network. In fact, didn't ENN run that ad a few days ago?"

"One time, and it was removed after that."

Jack laughed.

Carried looked at someone beside the camera who was motioning to her. "When we look at some of the video content The Times has produced lately, it has done nothing but smear Revision Communications, sabotage Monique Robinson's public image, and try to distract viewers from a murder. That's a pretty impressive streak, Jack. Why choose these subjects?"

Jack took a peek at the producer on site, who was motioning for Jack to be quick. "We decided to cover these stories because we felt they were of great public interest. Those were stories everyone in the world wanted more information about, and we were able to deliver. At The Times, we're always looking for interesting stories and new ways to present them."

Carrie winked at the producer in her studio telling her to end the interview. "Jack, we thank you very much for taking the time to speak with us this evening."

"It's been a pleasure, Carrie. I hope we can do it again soon."

"We'll be right back, here on ENN," Carrie said as the network cut to commercial.

ENN's crew started packing up their equipment, and Jack took the microphone off his shirt as he walked over to the kitchen, where he grabbed himself a cup of coffee.

Dustin walked into the kitchen and looked at him. "Thoughts?"

Jack drank his coffee. "Killed it."

"That was a no doubter, huh? Nothing but net?"

"That's correct, Dustin."

He walked out of the kitchen, while Jack stayed, continuing to sip his coffee. A few moments later, Jack walked back into his office to call Eric Peterson.

The phone rang five times before Eric picked up. "Hello?"

"Hey Eric, it's Jack, how are you?"

Eric was smiling from ear to ear. "Jack, I'm doing fantastic, how are you doing? That was a phenomenal display you just put on. I'm proud of you."

Jack leaned back in his chair. "Thanks, Eric. When the interview was over, I felt great about it. I'm glad you feel the same."

"Time will tell what our next move is, but I just got off the phone with David, and Horizon is thrilled with the job you did. Things are smooth sailing from here on out, my friend."

Jack breathed a sigh of relief. "That's nice to hear. Things have been pretty crazy. Hopefully the craze dies down, and we can get back to what we've been doing."

"Well, I'm not sure what's next for Horizon reactive content, but I think you deserve some time off. Go ahead and take the next two days off."

Jack sat forward in his chair. "Are you sure it's good for me to be out of the office now? Shouldn't I stick around just to make sure there isn't anything urgent that comes up?"

Eric tapped his desk. "No, I think you should take two days off. Take the time to relax and not think about work. If something comes up, we'll handle it, so don't worry."

"If you say so, boss."

"Good, enjoy the time off. You've been the perfect man for this job all along. I want you to know that. The Times has flourished, and it's all thanks to you, Jack."

Jack smirked. "Well, that's not true, it's been a team effort, and you've certainly been a big part of this company's growth. One man did not build The Times."

"Maybe, but you've played a significant role either way. Again, great job with the interview. You should take a moment to relish the hard work you've done."

"I will, Eric. I'm excited about what's in store for the future. It's going to be unforgettable."

Chapter 13

Over the course of the next week, outlets all over the country tried to make sense of the interview between Jack Strain and ENN. Most readers were still smitten with The Times, and the site continued to receive record-breaking traffic.

The harassing of Dustin, Cameron, and Jill stopped, and life for them had returned to normal. The Times continued publishing reactive content as they had before.

An opportunity arose for Horizon to sell their stake in the Newbury Stampede, and so the company sold it off to a soft drink company for a 10% profit.

Everything seemed to be going The Times' way until, "Hello and welcome to ENN, I'm Carrie Woodson. From an anonymous source, documents and files have been leaked revealing an intimate, working relationship between The Times and the telecommunications giant Horizon. In these files is evidence that the two companies colluded to further the business interests of both firms. The two have worked together to create dozens of videos, all with a specific agenda in mind. The videos, internally referred to as reactive content, covered topics such as the Dennis Lodge murder, Monique Robinson's life, and the Revision false advertising scandal. We'll have more on this story as it develops."

News stories erupted across the world, with The Times and Horizon up in arms about the leak. No one could scramble fast enough to provide a logical explanation to the irate public.

As soon as the ENN story ran, Jack called together his team into the conference room to discuss what happened.

Jack stood with his hands on the table. "Everyone sit down! Who in this room has been discussing reactive content outside our company?"

Dustin crossed his arms. "Do you really think any one of us would do this? Why would we jeopardize our own careers? I didn't do it." He pointed at Cameron. "I know you didn't do it. So let's step away from the cliff and put down the gun, okay, Jack?"

Jack slammed his fist on the table. "I'm the one who gets to decide who is innocent in this room. I'm the judge. I'm the jury, and I'm the executioner. Understand?"

Dustin shifted back into his seat and looked away from Jack.

The room was silent for a moment until it was broken by a call on the conference phone. Jack answered the phone on speaker. "Hello! This is The Times." He cleared his throat. "Jack Strain speaking."

"Good, so you heard about the leak," said a female voice on the other end of the call.

Jack took a breath. "Sorry for answering the phone that way. May I ask who this is?"

Dustin, Jill, and Cameron all stared at each other in uncertainty.

"It's Karen at Horizon. I just had an extremely unpleasant meeting here with my superiors. After conducting a brief investigation, we have determined the leak didn't come from inside Horizon, despite what ENN's report says."

Jack leaned forward and spoke closer into the intercom. "Well, you can be damn well sure that it wasn't us. Is that why you're calling?"

"Yes, that is why I'm calling. Look, the only people who had access to our contract files were upper-tier Horizon employees, including myself, and the four of you at The Times. We'd have no reason to leak anything. I just know there's a snitch among you and for the sake of The Times, they'd better come forward now."

Dustin moved his hand in a stopping motion. "As I already said to Jack, why would we leak this information? All of us love our jobs, we are exceptionally good at them, and we make a great deal of money. Why stopping playing when we're up by 10 and it's the bottom of the ninth?"

"Dustin, you're a great guy, but speak plainly here."

Jack looked at him. "Agreed, Karen. Dustin, no one here needs to be any more confused than we already are."

Eyes wide open, Dustin glared at him. "Jack, haven't you heard? There's a new ice cream shop down the street. Why don't you run down there and grab a scoop of shut the hell up?"

"Enough, Dustin. You are officially done talking on this phone call. I apologize for Dustin's behavior, Karen. You know how he is."

"Yes, I do know how he is, and I don't believe he leaked the information. Look, it's clear no one wants to speak up about this, and it's clear to me The Times leaked these documents. David Reid has given me full authority to terminate this agreement if I deem it necessary, and I'm afraid at this time we are going to have to do just that."

Jack fumbled and picked up the phone, now speaking with her directly. "Please don't, Karen. We've done so much with Horizon, and this is just a speed bump. You'll see, things can go back to normal once this clears up."

"That's just it, Jack. We can't go back to the way things were. All of you will be paid out for your efforts through today, per our agreement, but our contract is hereby terminated. Horizon will no longer have any affiliation with The Times. We wish you all the best," Karen said as she hung up.

Jack slammed the phone down.

Dustin, Jill, and Cameron all sat there in shock.

"How could things have gone this bad in a matter of hours? I should have gotten out of here when I had the chance," Cameron muttered.

Jack stood behind his chair and took a deep breath so everyone could hear it. He looked up at the three of them and walked out of the room.

Cameron put his hands up. "So what are we supposed to do now?"

Dustin got up from his chair. "I'll be back with beer."

"Bring a keg," Jill said.

In the meantime, Jack was back in his office, sitting in his chair. As he stared at the ceiling, his phone rang, causing him to nearly fall over. Finally regaining his bearings, he answered on the fifth ring. "Yeah."

"Hey, Jack, how are you doing?"

Jack fumbled to provide a response. "Eric? I'm good, how are you?"

"You sure about that? You don't sound like a man who is doing good."

"You're right, I'm not at all, but you know why that is, don't you?"

Eric let out a subtle laugh. "Of course I do, but I wanted to call and tell you it's not the end of the world."

"What? Of course it is. This leak is going to sink us. I'm looking at our traffic right now, and it is plummeting. People hate us."

"Ah, don't worry about that, my friend. We did all we could. There was eventually an end point to this thing with Horizon, and we reached it as we thought we would."

"So you're not upset right now?"

"No, I'm not. We made our money and Horizon did as well. I spoke with David and as far as he and I are concerned, this was a successful partnership. It has run its course, for now. You know how this goes and you know we will be fine."

Jack let out a sigh of relief. "It's just, our traffic is dying, Eric. How can you not be worried? Screw Horizon, our traffic is a disaster."

"Look, I know it seems bad, but I was given a heads up on the leak. I'll find a solution. The Times will be taken care of justly."

Jack put his hand on his forehead. "How does any of that help us though? Advanced notice about the leak doesn't fix what is happening to our traffic."

"Not another word about the damn traffic, Jack."

Jack sank in his chair.

"You and your entire staff go home for the rest of the day and don't think about work at all. Come back in tomorrow and be ready to get back to what we've been doing all along. Okay?"

Jack sighed. "You got it, we'll be ready."

While Jack was on the phone, Dustin returned to the conference room with three beers in hand. He took a seat and dealt out a beer to each of them.

Jill gazed into the bottle. "Beer feels like our only refuge right now."

Cameron leaned back in his chair and kicked his feet up onto the conference table. "Well, what a day, huh? We go from being the toast of the industry to being the roast. I'm not going to even ask what else could go wrong because I'm afraid there could still be more."

Dustin shrugged. "Trust me, we've emptied this bucket of crap."

Jill rolled her eyes. "Gross image, Dustin." She took a sip of beer. "What do you think we're going to do?"

Dustin nodded and pondered a response.

Cameron moved his beer. "You know, I think we've proven a lot over the past few years. I don't have any doubt that we will be fine as a company and wouldn't be surprised if another organization wanted to create another deal like the one we had with Horizon."

Dustin tilted his head back. "I guess it's possible, but would any company want to engage with us like Horizon did? Would we ever want to engage with a company like we did with Horizon? I hope none of you are forgetting about Dennis Lodge."

"Jeez, you're telling me! Wait, I take that back. I hope no company tries to do something like this again," Cameron said as he slouched in his chair.

Jill nodded. "Yeah, that was a joke. I'm surprised Jack isn't back from whatever he's doing. What should we do? It might not be a bad idea to just leave for the day. I don't think there's anything more for us to do."

Just before Dustin could reply, Jack walked back into the conference room and all three sat there in silence wondering what was about to happen.

"Go home, all of you."

Dustin and Cameron's jaws dropped at Jack's statement.

Jill sat forward in her chair. "Wait, are we fired?"

"No, of course you're not fired. Why in the world would the three of you be fired?"

Cameron leaned back in his chair. "Oh, I don't know, maybe the abrupt statement telling us all to go home with no follow-up."

Jack bit his bottom lip and agreed. "Yeah, you're right, I'm sorry for starting off with that. Allow me to fill you in on what happened while I was in my office."

"We're all ears," Jill said.

"I spoke on the phone with Eric and things are just fine. This was part of what he was expecting all along. He's not surprised, and he's not upset."

She laughed. "Really, Jack? He isn't angry one bit about what happened today?"

Jack shook his head and stood up straight. "No, not one bit, even though our traffic is third-world garbage. He knew this would happen and said we made the money we wanted to. Eric wants us to take the rest of the day off to not think about work. Come in tomorrow morning refreshed and ready to go."

Cameron nodded. "Okay. I know I can do that."

Dustin raised his beer. "Yep. Can do."

"Yes, I can as well," Jill said.

Jack was smiling from ear to ear. "I'm glad we are such a resilient bunch. See you tomorrow. Things will be just as they always have been."

They all got up from their seats and walked out of the room to gather their belongings.

That night, Eric and his wife Jessica put their kids to bed and then walked back downstairs into their living room to talk about the day's events. Jessica sat down next to Eric. "That was quite a day wasn't it, Eric?"

He laughed. "It sure was."

"So what's on your mind?"

Eric lifted his right hand. "Well, I'm thinking about selling The Times. Traffic is significantly down and we are way in the black as a company. It could be the right time to get out."

"Does this have anything to do with the person's offer you told me about this afternoon?"

"Yeah, it does. But given the situation The Times is currently in, there's just too much work to be done. Its reputation is destroyed. The best thing to do now would be to blow up the whole thing and start over, but I'm not real keen on online media anymore. The opportunity just isn't there any longer."

She brushed his hair back. "Just like that, you're willing to give it all up?"

Eric nodded with a smile. "Yes, but I am not giving anything up, just moving on to the next thing."

After Jack took time away from the office, he and his team were back to work. Traffic had never been so low for The Times.

The rest of the day went on until the routine was broken up by the arrival of Eric Peterson. He walked over to Jack's office and told him to gather up the entire company in the common area because he had an announcement to make.

Eric stood with his hands in his pockets and smiled at everyone. "My friends, what a journey this has been. We built this place from nothing, and it has become the most successful company of any online media firm in the world. Each of you should be proud of your successes, because this place is just that, a success."

Eric paused.

"In business, you have to make difficult decisions and put aside feelings of sentiment. I admire the work you've all done and am grateful for it. I've evaluated our current situation and have come to a logical conclusion."

"The Times has been sold."

The air in the room quickly escaped and people gasped at what they just heard. A few employees began crying.

"The individual I have sold The Times to is standing just outside the office. This is someone who deserves to own this company, and they alone will decide what its future will be. I led you all as far as I could, and so did Jack."

He pointed his left hand at the door. "Allow me to introduce to you the new owner of The Times…"

Everyone stood there, teetering on Eric's next two words.

"Karen Drove."

A paralyzing silence dominated the room, only to be broken by the sound of the front door opening and Karen walking in. She walked past the group and stood in front of them.

A handshake between the two was exchanged. "The floor is yours, Ms. Drove." Eric stepped away, leaving Karen standing alone.

People looked at her with a strong sense of uncertainty and fear.

"Hello, everyone. It's wonderful to see so many familiar faces. It's been a long time. Thank you for the introduction, Eric. It is a pleasure to be the new owner of The Times. I couldn't be happier."

Karen paced back and forth. "Many of you may be wondering about the future of the company, now that I'm the new owner.

While I can never erase time or fix matters of the past, I can control what does happen in the future."

She methodically looked around the room.

"This place has become a house of journalistic promiscuity and impurity. It has burned to the ground every single principle journalism used to stand for. The Times has changed the industry forever and for that, I will never forgive any of you, including myself."

Karen folded her hands.

"The problem with journalism is people got tired of doing the work that made it so respected and trusted to begin with. This industry got lazy and wanted to take the easy way out. They wanted to press the refresh button and hope things would look drastically different. Only it didn't, so people decided to accept the easy answer."

She held out her arms.

"The Times saw a marvelous rise of epic proportions, but all empires eventually crumble. I am here to cleanse this world of a disease. I am here to cut out the wound that has been festering in the heart of journalism for too long."

Karen paused for a moment. "I am here to close The Times."

"You all have until the end of the night to pack up your personal belongings. Tomorrow, this office will be vacated and closed."

After her speech, Karen walked over to Eric and thanked him once more. "It's been a pleasure doing business with you."

Eric smiled. "The pleasure is all mine, especially since the offer you made was something I couldn't turn down. Thank you, Ms. Drove."

Employees slowly filed out of the common space and returned to their desks to pack up.

Dustin walked over to Karen. "Interesting move, Ms. Drove. When you inherit over a billion, what's the first thing a person should do? Duh, spend a chunk of it and then flush that thing down the drain."

Karen laughed. "It's only a drop in the bucket."

"Different strokes for different folks."

"A fitting saying, Dustin, but you know what? I wanted to impact this world, and the journalism industry I love. I wanted to help it, and this is a first step in doing so. I'm sorry everyone is out of a job, but closing this place had to be done."

"I understand," Dustin said with a smile. "So, was it you who leaked those documents?"

Karen smirked back at Dustin and let a moment pass before replying. "Why would I have leaked that information? To send The Times spiraling down toward a crashing end? To put this place in the position where Eric could care less about it, therefore selling it to me? Dustin, leaking information, now why would I ever do that?"

"What was I thinking?" He rolled his eyes and then laughed. "At least dating a colleague is out of the picture. Want to grab some food later?"

"Sure."

Dustin winked at Karen as he walked away.

She walked into Jack's office and found him packing up his belongings. "Jack, do me a favor and round up the team in the conference room."

They all went into the room, and Karen sat in the seat Jack used to sit in. She was at the head of the table and addressed everyone. "I care about each of you. This decision was never about me getting revenge for being fired from The Times. I want you all to know that."

Jack had his arms crossed. "Please. I don't believe you for a second. Do you think this changes anything, Karen? Journalism isn't just going to reset because you decide to close us. Our way of doing business will continue to evolve. It's never going to die."

Karen looked at Jack with her hands folded together. "You're right. This isn't going to fix what is wrong with journalism. It will never again be what it once was, but that doesn't mean I can't still do something to help. All I ever wanted was to help."

Cameron nodded. "I think you're right, Karen. We all became lost in this journey to make money, and we forgot about our true purpose as journalists: to serve the public's best interest regardless of corporate and financial influence."

Karen looked at each of them. "So you all know, I knew exactly what Horizon wanted you guys to cover next. In fact, I knew the next five stories and trust me, I did each of you a favor. If you thought the Dennis Lodge story was bad, that pales in comparison to what you would have had to do next."

Cameron shifted in his seat, "I came here as a journalist, but I'm not sure what I've become. Even though you just fired us all, Karen, thank you."

"Thank you?" Jack yelled. "You're thanking the woman who just fired you. She is putting you on unemployment and taking away your livelihood."

Cameron shook his head. "I don't see it that way, Jack. This is a chance for us to redeem ourselves. This is a chance to redefine what our careers can be. Don't let this define who you are."

Dustin sat in silence with a smile on his face.

Karen stood up. "My friends, it's time to say goodbye and leave. I wish you all well in the future. May you go and do great things in life. If life should lead you back into the journalism world, think of this place and think of the things you've done. Remember to do the right thing, not the easy thing. Those decisions reveal who you truly are."

Final Thoughts

I nearly didn't write this book because I was scared. Scared that what I write may not be worthy of someone else's time. Scared that I may not have the capability to create a compelling world, interesting characters, and an immersive story. This is in no stretch of the imagination the best book ever written, but it's my petition to the journalism industry.

There is always more to tell, more to say, and more to reveal, but I feel this story does justice to a world that has lost its identity. The Internet is a powerful tool that can be used for great things, and horrible things. What people decide to do with it is the telling factor. I'm not sure if we'll ever know a journalism industry we can truly trust again.

I do have hope that those who are making decisions for the industry will one day rediscover the true purpose of what being a journalist is all about. I'm not sure what the world will look like when that happens, but I do know we all will be ready for it.

If you want to know what is native advertising and what isn't, I implore you to demand transparency and honesty from your chosen outlets. Do not be a sheep with the information you consume. Take charge of the information you consume in both print and online, and demand accountability. If there is nothing for companies to hide, then transparency will be simple and easy.

The final thoughts I leave you with are from a plane flight I had a long time ago. I had this message stirring in my head and had to write it down. This is what I believe is true of all of us, no matter who you are:

Every single one of us is a risk taker. You might not think of yourself as one or believe you are one, but rest assured, you are. You might not take risks with your job. You might not take risks with your life. But you are a risk taker. We all take risks on a daily basis. We take risks for friends. We take risks for family. We take risks for love. Don't ever be afraid to take a risk because as you go along in life, you begin to find out those risks have shaped who you are, and who you are not. So have some Faith and risk every chance you get. One day, you may be surprised with the person looking back at you in the mirror.

Acknowledgements

Throughout the course of the creation of The Decaying Pillars, there were a number of people who helped make this a reality.

First, I'd like to thank my Editor Kathleen Dale and her business partner Jeff Kirvin.

I've learned so much about writing from Kathleen than I would ever have discovered on my own. Jeff did an unbelievably great job of understanding my vision for the e-book cover and making it a reality.

They have been nothing short of a pleasure to work with and I'd recommend them to any writer out there.

For the print version of my book, I had the opportunity to work with talented graphic designer, Aldo Corona. Much like Jeff, Aldo was able to internalize the vision I had and illustrate it in an extremely powerful, precise way. I'd happily recommend Aldo to anyone looking for a standout cover.

I'm extremely fortunate to have met and collaborated with these three professionals along the path to creating The Decaying Pillars.

My thanks also go out to the few test readers I was able to convince to read my then jumbled up rambling. Thank you to my father, Tom Ruygrok, my mother, Robin Ruygrok, and my very good friends, Brooke Wylie and Jeremy Gendelman.

The feedback I received from each person was incredibly helpful in ensuring I was going in the right direction with the characters and story I had intended to create.

To everyone who helped make The Decaying Pillars a reality:

Thank You.

About The Author

Steve Ruygrok, a graduate of Ohio Wesleyan University, is a journalist who has been involved with the industry for years. He has worked in the gaming, music, film, tech, sports, spirits, performing arts, craft beer and consumer products industries. You can catch Steve on Twitter @DecayingSteve

www.ingramcontent.com/pod-product-compliance
Lightning Source LLC
Chambersburg PA
CBHW031318120626

46554CB00001BA/454